PHANTOM FROM THE PAST

With death now close behind him, Robert skiied for his life

Phantom from the Past

by Neil Gavin

Jarrold Colour Publications, Norwich

Cover design and illustrations by John McWilliam

Although this story is set in actual locations to be found on the appropriate maps, the characters exist only in the author's imagination. Any resemblance to persons living or dead is purely coincidental.

ISBN 0-7117-0358-2
© 1988 Jarrold Colour Publications
Printed and published in Great Britain by Jarrold and Sons Ltd, Norwich. 1/88

To the memory of my parents

CONTENTS

BEFOREHAND

At the end of the day you have to find your own identity; who you are, what you are. You alone can do this though others can help, just as Sean Moidart helps Robert in his search to discover the truth about himself.

Robert's quest is a long one which can neither be encompassed in one year nor in one book. *Phantom from the Past* therefore is just the beginning of his journey.

In recounting his adventures, his age-long battle with the Whisperer and later his evil cohorts, the Searchers, I have walked, cycled or driven down every street, over every inch of the Scottish countryside described in this book.

So when you read how Robert is trapped in the rushing waters of the River Braan, close to the Hermitage near Dunkeld, you can go there for yourself and see the acute peril threatening him.

In some instances I have taken liberties with descriptions, as with the old Perth Academy building in Rose Terrace, and allowed fantasy to take over from fact – but all in aid of writing a gripping account.

Robert's search, dangerous and exciting, lies ahead in the pages of this book. Why don't you share it with him?

Set out now as he seeks his true identity.

Footnote: I have taken only extracts from Fiona's diary because she is inclined to go on a bit! I have therefore selected the passages which seem to be of most interest and relevance.

Chapter 1
WORDS IN THE DARK

A portrait of Robert by Fiona

'We've got to tell the lad the truth. He has a right to it.' Robert Matheson, drowsing comfortably on the verge of sleep, heard the words coming up from the living-room downstairs. It was his father speaking.

'But why now?' That was his mother's voice.

'A damn fool question, Katie Matheson, and you know it.'

Robert had not intended listening but the urge to hear what they were saying was too great. He raised his head from the pillow and listened intently, his brain automatically registering that outside in the darkness snowflakes were drifting down. Tomorrow would be a good day for skiing.

'Just because it's his birthday tomorrow.'

'That,' declared his father in his clear, firm voice, 'is good enough reason.'

'But Bobby's only a boy.' Irritated, he wished his mother would not call him Bobby. A child's name.

'Robert is man enough to be told the truth.' Even upstairs he could detect the emphasis on the Robert.

His mother began to weep and Robert felt ashamed of himself for listening to his parents' conversation. He lay back on the pillow and gazed at the snowflakes, tried to shut out the sound of her weeping.

'Hugh, I don't want to lose him.'

His father tried to comfort her. 'You won't.'

'I will. I will.' Her voice, protesting, crescendoed.

Robert felt like rushing down and telling her . . . telling her what? That he would always love her? But increasingly these days he found it harder to express his true feelings towards his parents. His friends at school in the small town of Jasper only a few miles from the Canadian Rockies would have called him a 'mother's boy, sissy'. His sister Fiona, only eleven months younger, would understand how he felt. Could she be listening to this conversation?

1

He pressed his head more firmly into the pillow, closed his eyes and the voices below, now a murmur, grew gradually more distant. Just words in the dark.

Finally he slept.

A self-portrait by Fiona

Chapter 2
NO EXPLANATION

The snow had stopped when Robert awoke. Everything was still. Everything that is except the questions racing round in his brain.

He struggled into a sitting position, still bemused from sleep. What could they have been referring to? It had all sounded so mysterious. And would his father tell him today – his fifteenth birthday?

Down at breakfast that Saturday morning there was no answer. Mum and Dad both looked at ease with each other: from one a warm hug, from the other a manly hand on the shoulder and a happy chorus from both together – 'Happy birthday, Robert.'

There were cards from school friends and a tartan bonnet and a silver tie-pin in the shape of a claymore from Aunt Isobel Bervie Matheson in Perth, Scotland.

'Good old Aunt Isobel,' he exclaimed.

His mother smiled: 'One day soon your room will burst at the seams with all your Scottish paraphernalia.'

'We'll call it Mac's Museum,' added his father using Fiona's nickname for him.

'Fiona isn't up yet?'

'She's got a cold,' explained his mother. 'She knew you'd be disappointed, especially with the new fall of snow.'

'No ski-ing for her then.'

'I'm afraid not,' commented his father, pushing over the cereal packet while his mother poured out the coffee.

'Rough luck,' commented Robert. He had been looking forward to them skiing together and could not refrain from wondering if that meant the trip would be curtailed, or worse still, postponed.

His mother's pale face smiled at him. 'No, Robert, a promise is a promise and the three of us will be off to Shangri La in half an hour.'

Robert smiled with relief, then remembering that his sister was going to be stuck in the house, possibly in bed all day, asked, 'But will Fiona be – ?'

3

His father looked up from the sports section of the paper propped up in front of him. 'She's not dying. Just a bit miserable.'

'In that case,' replied Robert, 'I'll have a word with her before we go.' He paused. 'I know, I'll lend her my Scots chess set for the day. She'll like that.'

'Highlanders and Lowlanders in battle,' remarked his mother.

'That's the one. Aunt Isobel sent it to me.'

'As if I don't remember. Fiona played with it hour after hour for those two months when she had glandular fever.'

'And became junior champion when she returned to school,' added Hugh Matheson. He blew loudly into his coffee as he folded his paper with his free hand.

The headline was at an angle but Robert had no difficulty reading it. 'Fighting the Juggernaut.' He turned his head so that he could read the smaller type of the introduction.

'Every year the silent snow takes its mounting toll. This year is no exception. Already in the mountainous west of the United States there have been an estimated 100,000 avalanches, while in Canada . . .'

His father refolded the paper. 'Gloomy reading,' he remarked tersely as he scanned the article. 'They sure never learn.'

'How do you mean?'

'The number of avalanches in any one part of the world is pretty constant year in year out.'

'So?'

'Well,' said his father putting down the paper and giving the subject his full attention, 'why is it then that in the last thirty years the number of people killed in snowslides has multiplied by a factor of four?'

'I don't know,' said Robert.

His father was beginning to speak more like the civil engineer that he was. 'Every year more folk are taking to the hills and mountains with their skis and toboggans and they're venturing into avalanche active areas. In short, thousands upon thousands are facing hazards they've never faced before.'

'And bingo they're in trouble,' Robert put in a little flippantly.

'As you say, bingo!' His father gulped at his coffee with the habit of a man used to having to drink it in a hurry when out on location. 'All the same, even the experts are caught out sometimes. Avalanches are mean and nasty and they can break away without warning.' He paused. 'But take last night for instance.'

'Yes,' Robert leaned forward.

'All that snow driftin' down, nice big flakes they were. But they could be deadly under certain conditions. You see all you need is an accumulation of a couple of feet on one densely covered snowpack and that's enough to overload it. Rain and meltwater can also do the trick by releasing the bond with the layer of snow below.'

'Fine talk for a lad's birthday.'

'Education comes cheap in this house.' He shrugged easily. 'I'll give you more spiel in the wagon.'

Katie smiled. 'That means you'll be hearing more about how the scientists have classified hundreds of different kinds of crystal.'

'Hey, let's be accurate Katie. Eighty different kinds.'

By now Robert was halfway through a huge plate of ham and eggs. Still chewing he remarked, 'Joe and Bud Spilaud – both of them – they're always on about snow crystals.'

'Reckon they know what they're talking about,' said his father. 'Young Joe's shaping up well for an orphan.'

4

Robert smiled as he thought of his friend. 'Yes. He sure was having great fun with Tan in the snow yesterday.'

'You still hanker after a dog of your own?'

Robert nodded in response to his mother's remark.

'Sorry lad but that's something I'm not having here.'

'But, Hugh.'

'No, Katie. No dog. And that's final.'

Robert groaned to himself. If there was one thing in the world he wanted really badly – it was dog of his own. But mention the word 'dog' in the Matheson household and there was always an argument.

The conversation moved on to huskies, rescue teams and snow storms. Now his father was on to the dangers of poor quality concrete. Lots of talk but still no mention of what they were going to give him. Not a word, only a conspiratorial smile between them when they thought he was not looking. His mind went back to last night and the words, 'He's old enough to be told the truth.' But what truth?

He would ask Fiona if she had heard anything. But Fiona, lying in bed looking a little sorry for herself, said she had heard only a murmur of voices. 'You shouldn't have eavesdropped.'

'Trust you to say that,' he retorted. 'Anyway, it was only a few words.'

She dropped her moral tone. 'What about me, Mac? Did they mention me?'

He grinned mischievously. 'Who would mention an old thing like you?' he countered.

Fiona lifted her head from the pillow and very deliberately put out her tongue at him. 'You don't deserve your present for that.'

But Robert did not rise to the taunt and having placed the chessboard and pieces on the bedside table pretended to leave the room.

'Stop, you chump. It's over by the dressing-table.'

Robert liked surprises. Speculatively, he eyed the large blue papered parcel tied with gold ribbon.

'Three guesses.'

He weighed it in his hand. 'A book on the *Gathering of the Clans*.'

Fiona shook her head, enjoying herself.

'A handknitted scarf.' Said without too much enthusiasm.

Another shake of the head and now the green flecked eyes under the fringe of tousled fair hair were dancing.

Robert examined the parcel but there was nothing to indicate its contents.

'A – ' he hesitated, thinking hard – 'box of chocolates.'

Fiona sneezed and blew her nose.

He untied the bow, ripped open the paper and took the lid off a long narrow box. Inside there were black skiing gauntlets. He smelled them. Real leather. He looked up and met her eyes, realising that they must have cost her a lot of money. He swallowed hard.

'They're great – just great.' He wanted to say more, but couldn't find the words.

'I'll wear them today.' He crouched forward, knees bent, arms outstretched in the classic ski-ing position. 'Great.'

Fiona smiled. 'Great,' she repeated softly, then spoilt the effect by sneezing violently.

As he closed the door behind him, her voice was little more than a hoarse whisper. 'Give my love to Shangri La.'

Chapter 3
AVALANCHE

The mountain peak in the Canadian Rockies dissolved into a massive volcanic wave that tore down towards them

Robert's parents were waiting downstairs when he appeared in boots, parka and Aunt Isobel's tartan bonnet jammed down over his ears. His father was holding a pair of skis. They looked new, the runners waxed, unmarked. For a moment Robert did not guess their significance.

'Time you got yourself a decent pair of skis,' his father told him, a broad grin on his face. 'None of those kid things you've been using.'

His mother smiled. 'You are fifteen, after all.'

As she said the words Robert saw a look cross their faces, as if they had just remembered something. Last night's conversation? He studied the skis. 'Gee, they sure are top grade. Just top grade.' He used his favourite expression and saw his own pleasure reflected in their faces. His hands strayed over the wooden runners as he visualised himself racing down the long Shangri La run.

'Come on, move it, we don't want to spend all day here.' His father turned and they followed him outside and over towards the bright green estate wagon, their feet scrunching through the snow.

Robert felt content, happy until he looked back at his home and saw Fiona's face pressed against the window, a hand waving. Robert sensed that she was worried. Another of those premonitions. Surely not. What could happen today? Blue sky was the forecast with the promise of the sun warming everything up later.

Robert waved back before helping his father strap the skis onto the roof-rack. Then the back wheels were spinning slightly in the snow and the big station wagon began to nose out onto the main road.

Robert soon fell into a reverie broken by his mother saying, 'You don't think Fiona looked a little anxious just now?'

His father turned in the driving seat. 'I didn't see her.'

She smiled warmly at him. 'You wouldn't, but Robert – '

'Yes, I did,' he replied.

'I felt,' began his mother quietly, 'as if she were trying to tell us something.'

Commented his father breezily: 'More likely than not just saying goodbye.'

But Katie Matheson did not laugh and neither did Robert. It was almost as if Fiona were . . .

He closed his mind to his thoughts and stared out of the windows at the whitened landscape. They had left the town behind and in another few miles would be up in the mountains to the spot they called Shangri La, named after James Hilton's novel, which had caught Fiona's imagination.

His thoughts switched to the conversation at breakfast.

'Ever heard of an avalanche at Shangri La?'

'Not to speak of,' replied his father. 'But anything anywhere in the mountains can trigger off a snowslide. Old Bud Spilaud reckons that a trumpeter could set one off with a single blast.'

'Bud Spilaud would say that,' remarked his mother.

'Maybe, but they're hair-trigger killers and no mistakin'. An earth tremor, even a warm spell after a heavy fall of snow and you're in big trouble. In fact any overloaded slope can become a potential landslide.'

Robert digested this information in silence. It was his mother who spoke. 'I wish you'd never seen that article. It'll spoil everything.'

'We won't let it,' said Robert, not liking to see her upset.

When they emerged from the pine and aspen trees and swung round to park near the empty log cabin at the end of the road, with the blue sky arching overhead and the snow unmarked, it certainly looked like their secret place.

'Well here we are,' remarked his father, pulling on the handbrake.

'And not a soul to be seen,' she added, tying her hood under her chin and smiling round at him for a moment. 'That's what I love about it.'

'Me too,' remarked Robert then, remembering Fiona's white peaked face at the window added, 'Pity about Fiona.'

'Oh she's not much of a skier.' Typical remark from his father. Mother understood however. 'Maybe not, Hugh, but she loves the solitude of it all. Feeling it's her place.'

His father, understanding more than he sometimes revealed, said, 'But then it's all our secret place. It sort of belongs to us.'

He screwed up his eyes against the sunlight now glinting diamonds on the snow. 'A fine place to die.'

'What an odd thing to say.'

'Well, Katie, if you've got to meet your maker surely this is as good a place as any. It's clean and fresh.' His father, not given to making philosophical remarks, paused and Robert, letting his eyes absorb its bleak beauty, agreed.

'A man – '

'Or a woman,' his mother chipped in half-mischievously.

His father acknowledged her remark with a quick smile.

'A man or a woman could make a fresh start here. You know, set off like a pioneer into a new world.'

Perhaps, thought Robert, that was just what dying here would be like. Entering a new world - like a pioneer. Then, unbidden, into his mind came the memory of Fiona at the window and, yet again, his parents' conversation the night before. Just what did it mean?

Now they were unloading the skis, testing the straps, preparing for the long trudge to the ridge from which they always set off.

Once there, they buckled on their goggles and Robert flexed his fingers in Fiona's gauntlets. He looked up and caught his mother watching him. They smiled at each other.

Then they were off, slowly at first, bodies arched forward, curving into the turns. Now they were gathering speed, the wind whipping at their faces. Robert felt a surge of exhilaration and shouted aloud for joy. Trees raced by in a blur, the sky was a distant blue and his eyes were focussed on the ground immediately ahead. He struck a crisp section of firm snow and the skis ran like oiled silk with a faint hiss.

They had three runs that morning and paused for a haversack lunch back in the station wagon, because already the sun was dipping down on the horizon and clouds were shoring up in the west.

Hot Marmite from a flask revived them and and they munched steadily into mammoth hot dog sandwiches smeared thickly with mustard.

'Time for one more run,' his father was saying, 'before the weather breaks.'

His mother peered uncertainly out at the greying countryside and in that instant the wind keened through the trees and dusted the auto with a flurry of snow. 'Do you think that's wise?'

He smiled reassuringly, 'A short run and then we've got some talking to do.'

Her face tensed in profile. 'Must you?'

He put out his hand and rested it on her arm – an affectionate, reassuring gesture which Robert felt himself responding to as much as his mother.

'Yes, Katie.' His father slewed round in the seat and faced Robert. His eyes were wide set and blue. Robert observed in the driving mirror over his shoulder how green his own were in contrast.

'I've something I want to tell you, Robert, after this run.' His face tautened imperceptibly. 'Something important to you.'

Robert regarded his father steadily. Suddenly he wanted to know now, this very minute, not after another run – even on his superb new skis. 'Let's scrap the run,' he said in a slightly hoarse voice.

But his father was getting out of the station wagon and icy cold air was pouring in. 'After the run,' was all he said.

Up to the ridge they plodded and Robert was aware that his legs were tired.

They stood regaining their breath while, high above them, dark clouds gathered and the air grew colder by the second. Robert shivered as much from some primaeval fear as from the cold. Now there was a stillness as if time were suspended. His eyes roved the bleak landscape, pausing as they rested on the bright green of their station wagon. An osprey soared up from behind the pine trees on his right and on its mighty five-foot wingspan swooped low over the valley. It might have been a signal for it was then that they heard the first harsh crack high above them.

Silence. Another crack followed, louder and sharper this time, then a deep distant growl like thunder. Robert's flesh crawled and he looked in alarm at his parents. Shock was written over his mother's pale face and the skin stretched taut across his father's lean features. He looked behind him and Robert saw his face grow white as the snow. Robert could not draw his eyes from that face but something stronger impelled him to turn round.

At first he could see nothing – just fine tendrils of cloud, a puff and a whirl of snow like mist. But even as he watched, mesmerised, a great ridge of snow began to break away. The mountain peak seemed to be dissolving, reforming into a massive volcanic wave that tore down towards them.

'Katie, the north route.'

His mother looked wildly at them. 'No, Bobby first.' She shrieked the words.

Roughly his father turned her down towards the valley and safety and then he pushed her. She would have remained there if she could but already she was moving away from them, her skis at an awkward protesting angle.

8

What happened next Robert would remember with numbing horror all his life. She dropped a ski, tried to grab it and nearly lost her balance. But somehow she skied on, her free hand flapping frantically. Next she dropped her other ski and both arms were waving in the air.

'My God. My God.' All the agony of despair was in his father's voice. 'Robert. Now.'

Behind them was the horrifying roar of sound swelling and booming across the valley. Wind, viciously cold, tore at them. Robert bent forward, a final look at his father. In that moment between life and death he wanted to shout 'I love you.' But the words as always would not come and as his father swung down beside him, body crouched low, it was he who spoke.

'You're a Kinlochy now. Never forget it.'

Other words followed but they were torn away in the wind and flung about the valley in the great torrent of noise that enveloped them.

Instinct made Robert take the vertical more dangerous route and he was moving too fast before he could try and follow his mother. But his father was only yards behind her. Robert was veering further away now but he could not take his eyes off them.

Hugh Matheson, courageous man that he was, tried to force his ski-sticks into her hands but hysteria had overtaken her. Suddenly he straightened up and, with a magnificent challenging gesture to the world, threw away his ski-sticks and put his right arm round his wife's waist. Later, recalling it in slow motion, Robert somehow felt rather than saw that in that moment his mother regained her self-control for they seemed to put their arms round each other as if oblivious to the racing tornado of snow behind them. They were still moving very fast but not fast enough . . .

Robert had forgotten all about the crevasse to which his father had so often referred in the past. He must have been less than fifty yards from that treacherous cleft when the words came into his mind. 'Rob, turn south.' He reacted subconsciously, swinging down and over.

He missed the crevasse by a matter of feet and raced for his life towards the south route. Bending so low the ground seemed only inches from his face, the wind clawing at his cheeks, the dreadful surging torrent of white death behind him, he tore ever onwards. Down, down, down.

It must have been only the edge of the avalanche that caught him. Almost playfully it flipped him off the ground. Sky and trees were kaleidoscoping around him, whilst a blanket of snow was forcing its way into his mouth and up his nostrils. He closed his eyes and in the ensuing darkness tumbled and cartwheeled, his limbs feeling as if they were being wrenched from his body.

Chapter 4
BURIED ALIVE

Fiona, ill in bed, woke from her
nightmare – crying out his name

There was silence, not even a whisper of wind. His limbs were devoid of movement. It was as if he were in a cocoon – lifeless, yet alive.

Was this then death? Robert Matheson asked himself. But where were his parents?

The memory of them arm in arm skiing onwards to their own Shangri La filled his mind. Abruptly the mental image was blacked out. Panic filled him. The searing jagged kaleidoscope of himself being flung into the air by the avalanche superimposed itself on his thoughts.

Robert was buried alive in Shangri La . . .

That was the moment he began to struggle, to fight for his life. Gradually he became calm and started to think out the problem. Suffocation was the immediate threat. Slowly he managed to move his head while forcing down on the snow beneath himself with his arms. But was the ground actually beneath him? Might he not be lying face down? That started the feeling of panic again but somehow he overcame it. Now his head had moved, just a centimetre or two but it did move. Yes. He began to wriggle his shoulders but at first nothing happened and the overpowering feeling of claustrophobia overcame him. He could not see and could hardly breathe.

God save me! He was shouting the words but they were soundless, just frantic scratches of thought across the inner membranes of his mind. No sound came.

Robert began to feel drowsy as a feeling of lethargy crept over his limbs. Perhaps it was all too late. He made one last effort to move his head.

The snow loosened round his face. Desperately he worked his head from side to side. The snow pressed down with less force on his face. Then he found he could breathe though he was still in total terrifying darkness.

He heaved his head up and, like a periscope, his nose broke the surface of the snow and he could breathe properly.

He managed to lift his head and as the snow fell away from his mouth he gulped in the air and his heart hammered against his chest. He was alive. But for how long? The bleak dusk of winter was falling. Soon it would be dark: what then were his chances of surviving a night in the icy cold?

Robert felt deeply afraid. If – if his parents – somehow he could not bring himself to think of them as dead. His mind twisted away from the thought so that subconsciously he began to rephrase what he was thinking. If he died then who would look after Fiona?

Thinking of Fiona and then of the need to find his parents invested him with fresh determination to escape. And so he began his struggle but, even as he did so, the wind veered sharply and with it came the snow – not gentle soft Christmas-card flakes but vicious thick blinding flakes that settled on his head and began to build up around it as if trying to bury him again.

Exhaustion, and the sheer weight of the snow on his limbs began to take its toll and gradually he weakened.

Lying still, eyes closed, his breathing became slower and slower.

★★★★★

The morning had dragged by for Fiona, her nose stuffed, her head aching. A thermos of hot lemon and blackcurrant left by her mother and a dose of paracetamol had helped lessen the misery.

Fiona looked across longingly at the large framed colour photograph of her Shangri La taken by Robert the previous winter. Her heart ached to be out there, absorbing the remoteness of it all. She was the first to admit that she was not a great skier but one of the gentle lower slopes was ideal for her.

She dozed, took another drink and more paracetamol before falling asleep. Perhaps it was the image of the photograph on her mind but almost at once her eyelids began to flutter. She moaned and stirred restlessly as if in a fever.

It all began as a dream, a gentle enjoyable dream. There she was standing overlooking Shangri La, the green station wagon near what they called the south run, her parents skiing together, arm in arm. That seemed strange. And where were their ski sticks? Robert was hurtling down the south run.

The gentle dream had become a nightmare. A vast towering wave of snow was thundering down on them. Robert, crouching lower, was travelling faster than ever but the avalanche was catching up on him. She wanted to shout, to warn him, but she stood in her nightmare on the ridge watching helplessly. Her sense of perspective shifted and she found she could no longer see her parents.

Her eyes were back on her brother. 'Rob,' she screamed, calling him by the name she had used since she was a young child whenever she wanted to warn him of danger. Spelt backwards it stood for 'Beware of Rat'. The sound of her own screaming woke Fiona. The scream echoed round her bedroom and she gazed wildly about her.

Fiona sobbed aloud. She had to do something. But what? And why? She looked out of the window. Dusk was falling. Snowflakes were swooping past. An image of her brother flashed across her mind, of a flowing torrent of snow growing in velocity and height pounding down the mountainside, gaining remorselessly on the three skiers . . .

Fiona closed her eyes to the scene, but it was so horrifyingly vivid that it had etched itself on her mind.

She could stand it no longer: out of bed, pulling on a thick dressing-gown, seizing a huge scarf from a drawer and winding it round her throat, she ran downstairs to the phone. There was one person who could help – Bud Spilaud, born in East Europe and proud of it, prouder still of his work in helping protect a twenty-five-mile stretch of the Canadian Highway from avalanches.

If anyone knew anything about the terror of avalanches then he did. Years with a rescue team before he came to live in Jasper had equipped him with an in-depth experience of how to tackle the problem of conducting a search for people buried under the snow. The Spilaud family even had an Alsatian dog, improbably named Vortex.

With nervous fingers Fiona dialled the Spilauds' number and waited while it rang and rang, but there was no answer.

★★★★★

It was a sharp, jagged snow crystal which stopped Robert from falling into the deep white sleep of death as he lay trapped in the snow. It tickled his nose and made him sneeze.

Robert laughed aloud. How ridiculous it was for him, lying there with the snow compacting and freezing hard around his limbs to sneeze. It was different for Fiona: she had a cold and was warm in bed – just the place for a good sneeze. With renewed determination he began to move his head to and fro, to and fro.

He knew the danger of what was happening to him. He had read of so many cases of people being frozen to death in only a few feet of snow. There was even the case in Colorado of a skier trapped only ankle deep being forced to step out of her ski boots to escape.

All the time the snow was falling, building up on his head.

Worse lay ahead. Darkness was coming down like a huge cloak enveloping the countryside. Soon he would be able to see nothing and be seen by no one.

Fiona felt like crying out in frustration as she listened to the phone ringing. Still no reply.

She dialled the fire brigade but the number was engaged. She slammed down the receiver and glared at the phone. Then she remembered that if she just let the phone ring eventually it would be redirected through to the fire brigade control room as was the normal procedure in an emergency.

But for some inexplicable reason she did not redial the fire brigade. Instead she redialled Bud Spilaud's number and waited and waited.

Perhaps a minute went by as she stood there in her dressing-gown and thick scarf, the only sound in the otherwise silent house the ringing of that distant phone.

Then she heard it. A loud sneeze. A very loud sneeze. Had she sneezed or was it just something she had heard in her mind?

Laughter. But she was not laughing and there was no one near her.

Desperately she concentrated her thoughts on Robert but no mental image appeared: only the sound of a sneeze and laughter.

Reluctantly she began to lower the receiver.

'Hallo, hallo.' The accent was still thick mid-European, the voice strong and friendly. Fiona could have cried in relief. 'Mr Spilaud. It's Fiona.'

'Ach yes, I recognise you. I haf just come in the door and I hear the phone – '

Fiona interrupted in a torrent of words. 'I'm worried. Mum and Dad and Robert have not returned from skiing. They should have been back now.'

'It is becoming dark. Perhaps they are taking it slow in the snow.'

'It's not just that.'

'*Ja?*'

Then she burst out, 'I had a dream, a nightmare about an avalanche and it was tearing down the mountainside. They were skiing trying to escape.'

'*Ach so*, a dream you say.' Relief was evident in his voice, disbelief in the urgency of the situation. 'Well, my *liebchen*, do not worry your sweet head.'

Fiona almost screamed at him: 'But you don't understand. It was so real. I have these –
feelings sometimes.'

'And they are true?'

'Yes,' she hesitated, then added truthfully, 'sometimes.'

There was silence as Bud Spilaud thought about this.

'Please, Mr Spilaud. You are the one person I know who could help. You have had
all that experience protecting the Highway. You used to tell me all about how you had
howitzers.'

'105 millimetre they were. So you remember.'

Fiona was desperate but she felt she was catching his interest.

'Yes and you had dynamite too so you could blow away the small avalanches before
they grew too big.'

Perhaps he was testing her, for he interrupted brusquely, 'And how would howitzers
and dynamite help me find your parents and Robert?'

Now she was close to tears. 'I just meant you had experience,' her voice tailed off
lamely. 'But you've saved people from dying in the snow. Dozens of them.'

'Fifty-six,' he corrected then added, with sadness in his voice, ' and one dead child.'

'If Robert and my parents are in danger then you could save them.'

'Today I feel old.' He was being both stubborn and stupid, she thought.

'But you're not old, Mr Spilaud. You'll never be too old to help people.'

'No, you are right. If this is a wild goose chase . . .'

'Please, please hurry.'

'Fifteen minutes, *liebchen*.' The phone went dead. She put down the receiver and
found that she was shivering violently – from her cold or reaction she did not know, but
now she would have to dress.

Chapter 5
RESCUE

The rescue party fought their way through snow and darkness to find the buried figure

S hivering violently, Fiona hurried upstairs and with shaking fingers began to dress in her thickest clothes.

Outside it was already dark but she could see the snowflakes falling. They were so beautiful but so deadly for anyone out on the windswept slopes of Shangri La.

For all her anxiety and her illness she was thinking clearly. On with the kettle – they would need hot liquid and strong tea would be as good as anything. Warm blankets. A torch.

Fiona had hardly finished gathering it all together when there was a loud knocking at the door and there was Bud Spilaud with his son and two neighbours, their clothes whitening in the snow.

'You are ready, *liebchen*,' he said and his eyes swiftly took in her preparations. '*Ach*, that is good. We will need these things.'

'But father, we have them already,' cut in his son.

But Bud Spilaud knew the wisdom of allowing her to do something positive. He gestured to his son to be quiet and, introducing his two neighbours, led them into a large pick-up.

Fiona squeezed onto the bench front seat.

'You have the fever, you must wrap up carefully,' muttered Bud Spilaud crunching the gears.

It was an eerie journey with the driving snow, dazzlingly bright in the headlights, racing in on the windscreen.

As they drove Fiona explained again what had happened, told them exactly where Robert and her parents would be.

'They should be okay,' said Mr Spilaud. He paused, his hands tightening on the wheel as the vehicle began to slide on a sharp bend. 'So long as there is no snowslide. That would make it very difficult.'

'But father is experienced.'

Mr Spilaud nodded. 'That is so, but the snow up there – it is,' he paused, searching for the right word, ' – dicey.'

The sound of that simple slang word somehow started Fiona's teeth chattering uncontrollably. Bud Spilaud glanced anxiously at her.

'You should be in your bed.'

'Robert and my parents – they need my help.'

'I know, I understand.' His voice was gruff, sympathetic in its gutteral way.

In the back the other two men and Carl were talking together in an undertone.

Gradually they fell silent as the snow grew thicker and Bud had to slow down to take the corners. Even so there were times when the big pick-up would begin to slither into the nearside ditch and he had to struggle to keep it on the road.

The heater was full on and Fiona dozed a little. Bud's voice woke her.

'Where now, *liebchen?*'

She opened her eyes, peered blearily through the windscreen.

'To the right by the pines and cotton trees.'

'*Ach*, that I know,' he grunted and slewed the vehicle round onto the snow-covered track.

'There's the station wagon,' Fiona shouted as the headlights picked up the other vehicle.

Everyone leaned forward, peering ahead to look for any sign of the Mathesons.

'They must still be out on the slopes,' said Fiona, alarm in her voice.

Bud grunted to himself, 'That is what I fear.'

'It will not be easy,' said Carl and there was a subdued chorus of 'No, it won't be,' from the other two men.

Bud Spilaud looked hard at Fiona as he turned off the engine. 'I worry about you, *liebchen*. You should not be out here.'

'I have to be.'

He nodded. 'I know. Come quickly then and show us the way.'

Outside in the wind and the snow their eyes nevertheless rapidly adjusted to the fading gloom. But there was nothing to bring them comfort. Snow, snow and more snow. Deep and treacherous.

Fiona strained her eyes. What was that in the distance? A blob of colour in the snow.

'The lights. Put them on full beam,' she cried.

Bud Spilaud, back in the car in an instant, flicked the headlights on. Just visible in the distance was a brightly-coloured tartan bonnet.

The men plunged knee high into the snow and the wind whipped wickedly at their faces. Fiona valiantly tried to keep up with them but she soon fell behind and Carl took her by the arm to prevent her from falling.

A faint cry was heard ahead, half-lost in the storm. 'It is Robert.'

Fiona gasped. Oh, pray to God, he was alive. Please. Please. She mouthed the words soundlessly, imploring God to come to their aid. He must be alive.

Alive. Alive. Alive. The words hammered through her mind forcing out the dreadful thought – dead, dead . . .

Bud Spilaud was using a shovel with long careful strokes. The other two were bending down in the snow.

Fearfully, stumbling as she went, Fiona came upon them and gazed down at the face of her brother.

His eyelids, coated in snow, half opened and then winked. Was that possible? His voice mouthed words they could not hear in the storm. Fiona bent down. 'Robert, you're alive.'

'Father and mother, down the north run – landslide caught them.' His eyes closed, his voice faltered with the effort then he roused himself. 'You must save them . . .' Robert was unconscious.

For Fiona that February night became a nightmare.

Bud Spilaud and his neighbour Harry Marks staggered back to the wagon with Robert's inert body. The searching for her parents along the north route proceeded in what was rapidly becoming a blizzard, accompanied by the constant high keening of the wind. It was as if the elements had conspired to defeat their efforts and those next morning of a fully-fledged mountain-rescue team. But she knew nothing of that at the time.

Later, when she came to in her own bed with their neighbour Sue Madison looking after her, her first question was of Robert.

She hardly dared voice the words. 'How is he?'

Sue's face smiled briefly. 'He'll be fine. Still in hospital he is but you'll have him back home in a couple of days, to be sure.'

For a moment Fiona relaxed gratefully in the warmth of her bed. That was wonderful. She thought of the absurd-looking tartan bonnet, realised that it had probably saved her brother's life and sent a prayer of thanks to Aunt Isobel in Perth.

But then a shadow fell across her mind and instinct told her that she need not ask after her parents. But she did so all the same.

Sue sat down abruptly, twisting her hands awkwardly together. 'I don't know how to tell you, Fiona.'

'Oh no.' Fiona cried out before she could stop herself.

'Well, not definitely, I mean, well,' Sue was stuttering. 'What it is . . . they haven't actually found your mum and dad.'

'Buried in the snow?'

'I'm afraid so. There can be no hope now.'

Fiona felt desolate, more alone than she could ever remember. She began to shiver. Later she cried.

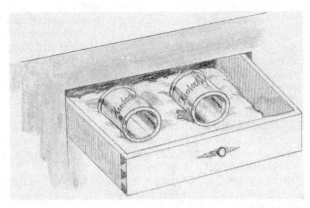

*The two rings bore the names Fiona
Kinlochy and Robert Kinlochy*

Chapter 6
KINLOCHY

F iona recognised the handwriting instantly. 'A letter to both of us from Aunt Isobel in Perth.'

Robert, dejectedly going through his father's belongings, looked up. 'Read it, Sis.'

She opened the envelope.

> My dear Fiona and Robert,
> I was deeply distressed to learn of your mother's and father's tragic deaths.
> Hugh was a dear brother to me and I know a fine father to you and I share your great personal sense of loss.
> I have never been one to believe in uprooting young people from their homes – I remember how we as a family had to live in Stafford when my father was working there and how we all longed to return to Arisaig – however, I think it would be for the best if you came and lived here in Arisaig with me. I should hope you would come to regard it as your own home.

At this point Fiona started to cry. 'Oh Robert,' she wailed.

He put his arm round her rather awkwardly to comfort her, 'Come on, Sis. Read the rest of it.'

'I can't,' she cried. 'You read it.'

Robert shrugged unhappily and started to read the letter written in a large bold hand.

> I should have written earlier but I have been away on a teaching second-ment this term and have only today received the news.
> I tried to phone you, of course, but the Canadian operator told me your phone was out of order. However, I shall be in touch shortly – never fear.
> I am afraid this has all been a terrible time for you both but I am confident that with your heritage you will come to terms with what must be a fundamental change in your life.

17

"Heritage", what for heaven's sake can that mean?' asked Fiona.

'Search me, unless she means that Dad and Mum were such fine people and had a long Scottish tradition behind them . . .' His voice trailed off.

'But that doesn't really solve what's to happen to us.'

Robert went and gazed out of the window at the garden and thought how much there would be to do to it just to keep things in order. 'That's right. But we could stay on with the Madisons. They've been swell and Sue Madison said they'd just love to have us.'

Fiona reflectively chewed at a strand of fair hair. 'I guess that's not a bad idea, Mac. So we say no thanks to Aunt Isobel.'

'I dunno – what I mean is not yet. I want time to think.' He grinned apologetically at her. 'We want time to think.'

'Okay. No rushing into things.'

Robert scuffed a shoe against the carpet and rubbed the palm of his hand against his chin, hoping to find the first fine traces of stubble to be shaved – all signs that he was undecided.

'Give over, Mac, what's biting you?'

He rubbed his chin more fiercely. 'I just can't fathom out Dad's last words – Remember you are a Kinlochy now. Those words have been churning round in my mind. But they make no sense. It doesn't figure, Sis.'

'It may not figure, Mac, but I know you too well. You won't quit till you've got the answer so let's keep worrying at it – but a little at a time.'

'That's a deal.'

At that moment the phone rang. Robert answered. 'It's the lawyer,' he told Fiona, his hand over the mouthpiece.

His voice held a harsh Scottish timbre which grated on Robert's ear. 'I think it's time I saw you and your sister about your affairs,' he was saying. 'There are a number of matters I should like to clear up.'

Robert was silent, wondering what these matters could be.

'Of course the terms of your father's will are perfectly straightforward. But they are not to be discussed over the phone. I should like therefore to suggest a meeting.'

'Yes, when?'

'My diary is unfortunately booked up for today and tomorrow.' There was a pause and Robert wondered why there should be any sense of urgency. After all it was some time since his parents had died and until now the lawyer had made no effort to contact them.

'What about 10.30 a.m. the day after tomorrow.'

'Sure, that'll be okay by me. My sister and I will come down to your place then.'

The lawyer's harsh voice cut in abruptly. 'No need for that, Robert. I should like to drop in on you. Gives me an opportunity to verify if there are any documents I should be seeing.'

Puzzled, Robert replied, 'See you then at 10.30 a.m.'

He put down the phone and looked across at where Fiona was standing listening.

'I don't know what to make of that. He sounded anxious to come over. Seemed a bit sudden.'

'Very sudden. It's as if someone has sort of told him he should be seeing us.'

'My thought exactly. But why?'

That evening they again had supper with the Madisons, Sue clucking sympathetically over them, husband Len telling her not to worry over how much they ate. The atmosphere inside was warm and comfortable, while outside a cold wind blew against the windows.

18

Their daughter Madge, Fiona's best friend, was going out with a boyfriend so Robert and Fiona decided to return home early for a change.

Sue, however, was anxious as always that they should stay the night. But after the first few days Robert had said that in the meantime they had to get used to sleeping on their own in the house. What had happened was that Madge came over for the night and then they all trooped back to the Madisons for breakfast. The arrangement had worked well but now Robert was determined to see to what extent they could manage on their own. Only then would he decide whether they should accept the Madisons' offer to live permanently with them.

The goodnights over, they left the house, hunching their shoulders against the wind, and quickly made their way the short distance to their own house. The single light which they had left on shone welcomingly through the window.

'It is home, Sis.'

Fiona nodded, biting her lip. He fiddled with the key for a moment and then it was in the lock and the door was open and they were home.

Robert switched on the electric fire though the house was reasonably warm thanks to the central heating, on at low.

'Cocoa, Mac?'

'Sure. You make it just like – Mum. Heck, when do we ever get used to it?'

Fiona tried a lopsided smile. 'Don't be silly, stupid. Think of our heritage.'

Recalling Aunt Isobel's word in her letter, Robert smiled. 'Sure, our heritage. We'll drink to that.'

Afterwards, they talked about the future – a future that they would have to share with either the Madisons or their aunt. Either way most of the family possessions would have to be sold. Robert was practical about it, Fiona hopelessly sentimental. But they agreed reluctantly to keep only the small things plus an old desk which had come over from Perth originally.

Fiona fetched down from their parents' bedroom a lovely old paperweight which they had treasured. It was of an unusual design with miniature claymores forming an intriguing design. The base was deep blue like lagoon water under a clear sky.

'I think really it belongs to your Scottish collection,' remarked Fiona.

Robert took it in his hand, held it to the light and watched it glimmer and sparkle. Yes, it would go well in his collection. But he caught Fiona's eyes and realised how much she would like to keep it. 'A nice idea, Sis, but I reckon you should keep it in custody.'

The elfin features lit up. 'Oh, that's magic of you.'

Then they looked in the old desk drawers which opened and closed with smooth precision. Robert fingered a bundle of letters, hesitantly, wondering if they should read them, give them to the lawyer or throw them away. He recognised a recent one as coming from Aunt Isobel and out of curiosity opened it.

The very first words caught his attention.

Dear Hugh,

There's no question about it: of course, you should tell Robert on his birthday. He has every right to know. So too has Fiona for that matter. A sweet child from all that you have written about her but well able to cope with the truth at her age.

I note that from your letter you would tell them at the end of the day after you've gone skiing. Again I think that is an admirable idea but don't let your dear wife dissuade you.

19

The letter then dealt with local gossip and a friend's son, Pete, who in some obscure way had managed to link up his computer so that he could communicate with the lawyer.

You'll remember that Pete's father and he were great friends before he emigrated to Canada. I believe you said once that he was your lawyer.

But by that stage Robert had more or less lost interest and was busy trying to work out what Aunt Isobel had meant.

'I can't figure it at all,' he said.

'It must have been important if Dad had written to Aunt Isobel about it.' Fiona chewed the end of a strand of hair. 'I'm not a child, even if I am sweet,' she remarked at last.

Robert grinned. 'Neither of us are children. We're – we're adolescents – teenagers both of us.'

He looked again at the letter. 'What about asking the lawyer about this business – Kinlochy and all that?'

But two days later when the lawyer, lean, sharp-suited, probing eyed, arrived and gave the impression of wanting to – as Fiona later put it – 'snoop' round the house, Robert decided not to mention the subject.

Muttering something about having to check that all was in order, he began to peer into everything after having gone into the details of the will.

He showed a special interest in the old desk. 'I must ensure that there is no question of a later will negating the terms of the will lodged with me.'

Robert looked puzzled. 'I don't follow your meaning.'

The lawyer grimaced. 'There are occasions, you understand Robert, when people decide – just on the spur of the moment – to make out a new will. For reasons best known to themselves they lodge it in some safe place in their own home instead of entrusting it as they should do to their family lawyer.'

'Gee, I'm sure certain that Mum and Dad wouldn't do that with you. Why they've known you for years.'

The lawyer smirked, preened himself. 'Long-established clients they have been. Knew your father back in the old country.'

It was on the tip of Robert's tongue to ask him then why he had not contacted them earlier. But he refrained.

'No valuable *objets d'art*?' the lawyer asked, with what Robert recognised as a deliberately casual tone of voice.

He was going to mention the paperweight but Fiona caught his eye and instinctively he knew that she did not want him to say anything. His silence evoked a look of suspicion on the lawyer's sharp features.

But at last what Fiona was to term as the 'Inquisition' was over and, looking disappointed, the lawyer finally took leave of them. 'I'll be back if anything comes to mind,' were his final words. And in Robert's ears they sounded more of a threat than a promise though for the life of him Robert could not tell why.

'You know something, Sis.'

'What?'

'I reckon he was after something.'

She turned puzzled green eyes on him. 'Like what?'

'I dunno. That's the trouble.'

'He sure rummaged around that old desk all right.'

'Yeah, you can say that again. And that's just what I'm going to do.'

Robert found more than he bargained for. Indeed the discovery he was to make changed their whole lives.

20

But first it was Fiona who discovered something. A brown manila envelope, the kind found in thousands of offices all over the world. But this one was different because printed in green ink on the front were the words THE KINLOCHY CLUE.

She stood looking at the envelope. Her hand trembled.

'Hey there, what's got you?'

Fiona shook her head in bewilderment. 'I can't guess. It's weird though.'

Robert took the envelope from her but felt nothing. He slit it open with an old pocket knife Aunt Isobel had once sent him years earlier. Inside was a small piece of faded paper, almost like parchment. It was creased and there was a smudge from a finger in the bottom right-hand corner.

> *When weight of paper is like stone*
> *and flashing claymore is all alone*
> *a myriad patter of pinpoints green*
> *creates a Scottish map that must be seen.*

They looked at it together.

'Well, Robert, what do you make of that?'

He rubbed his chin reflectively for a moment. 'I've haven't got a clue.'

She laughed. 'That was quick,' she said pointing to the words on the envelope.

'But it is a clue all the same.' He shrugged. 'Let's look some more and see what we can come up with.'

This time it was Robert who found it. He had noticed that the central drawer was not so deep as the ones on either side, so when he pulled it out too far, spilling the contents on the floor, he paused before replacing it. Fiona started picking up the letters and bits and pieces that accumulate in a drawer over the years. Robert for his part put his hand inside the aperture to check the runners for the drawer and right at the back felt a small wooden dowel to the right.

He pressed the dowel. There was a faint click.

'I've found something.' His voice was excited. 'It feels like a secret drawer.'

And so it was. A beautifully made drawer, lined in some kind of velvety material. Inside there were jewel boxes covered in dark green leather, cracked and scored with age. Gold hinges and a gold strip round each where they opened completed the impression that they held something valuable.

'Now just what have you got there, Mac?'

This time there was no mistaking the vibration in her hands as Fiona held one of the two boxes. Fascinated, he watched those slender trembling fingers open the box.

Inside there was a beautifully hand-wrought napkin ring made of antique silver, heavily scrolled and with two names engraved in large flowery writing.

Fiona Kinlochy.

She let out a cry of startled pleasure.

He did not wait a moment longer but also lifted back the other lid. There was an exact replica but this time with the name *Robert Kinlochy.*

Inside each ring next to the hallmark was the date of birth. So there was no doubt about to whom they belonged.

Now they were both silent, standing by the old mahogany desk, holding the rings in their hands, feeling the age and the beauty of them. Feeling too perhaps something else: a silver link with the past. A link that invested them each with a new identity.

The riddle of those words in Aunt Isobel's letter was suddenly explained. The explanation behind those cryptic last words of his father. 'You're a Kinlochy now. Never forget it.'

Finally Robert spoke. 'So we were adopted.'

Fiona bit her lip. 'We – we must have been orphans then.'

He nodded. 'Sure orphans – just orphans. And that's what we are again.'

Fiona put the napkin ring against her cheek. 'And the future, Mac. Where to now?'

Robert never so much as paused. 'We're going to Scotland.'

Chapter 7
TOUCH-DOWN

Thousands of miles later, there she was
waiting to welcome Robert and Fiona

The huge Boeing 747 powered by four turbo-jet engines had left Montreal nearly six hours ago and was cruising above the Atlantic at a steady 600 mph.

Robert and Fiona had eaten and slept and eaten and slept but now excitement had taken over and they were alternately chatting together or tensely silent, longing for Scotland to come into view.

'Oh, Fiona, I can hardly wait to land.'

'Nor me. I wonder – '

'Yes?'

'What do you think Aunt Isobel will really be like?'

They had asked each other that question many times over the last few months and were now a little apprehensive. After all, she was going to be their guardian; they were going to live in her house, share it as their home from now onwards; go to the school in Perth she chose for them. Oh so many things were going to change and all in a few hours' time . . .

Fiona fished around in her handbag for the now dog-eared photo that Aunt Isobel had sent them of herself – 'so you can recognise me easily at Prestwick airport,' she had written in her big bold handwriting.

The two heads were close together as they studied it.

'She is tall.'

'Nice, tweedy outfit but a bit old-fashioned, don't you think?'

Robert sighed. 'It doesn't tell us very much does it?'

'No, I know what you mean. We can't really see her expression. And that's what counts.' Fiona wrinkled her nose, and pushed back a stray lock of hair. 'So long as she is kind and – just a little motherly.' Now she blinked back a tear and Robert gulped. In that instant the image of their parents skiing down the long windswept slope with the great wave of snow leaping up behind them came into his mind. Had they still been alive then he and Fiona would have been at home in Canada – still Mathesons in name and in heart . . .

He looked at his sister. 'We'll just have to wait – '

'And see.'

What they did see quite shortly, as the Boeing began to make its long descent, was in the distance the outline of an island – Arran, the captain informed them over the speaker system. Tantalising glimpses of the island bobbed in and out of view then were lost to sight. But in those critical moments their thoughts were focussed on the Ayrshire coast with the Atlantic waves flowing up on the long stretches of beach.

Now they were coming in to land at Prestwick Airport. Touch-down and a slight bump. The screaming of tyres. The roar of the engines with the jets in retro-thrust. Hands tightly gripping the arm rests.

Then the plane was stopping, turning, finally coming to a halt not far from the airport buildings. Now the tension was almost unbearable as they sat strapped into their seats waiting, waiting.

Finally the doors were open, the smiling airhostess had handed down their coats from the lockers, and they were struggling to their feet, Fiona complaining that her green cord trouser suit had got all 'mussed up'. The long tedious push and shove down the corridor followed and then the first breath of Scottish air. Robert paused on the top of the gangway and breathed in deeply. So this at last was his true homeland . . .

He looked at his watch: nine fifty and Calgary was eight and a half hours away – light years away so far as he was concerned.

Fiona was waiting for him, her hair blowing in the light morning breeze. They walked across towards the compact-looking airport buildings, each wondering anew just what Aunt Isobel would be like. They found out sooner than expected because immigration and customs caused no delays.

There was no kissing or hugging, just a firm handshake and a smile of welcome and appraisal from the tall, slim figure in her blue check tweed suit. This, thought Robert, was a real no-nonsense lady, but for all that her auburn hair was softly waved, her voice softly accented in a way that he found attractive.

'It'll have been a long night for you both.'

Fiona gushed out of nervousness. 'We were too excited to sleep much. The flight just went on and on and on.' Her voice faded when she realised she was going to 'run on' as her mother used to put it.

Robert was quiet, trying to be adult as if flying the Atlantic were a routine matter for him. 'We're sure glad to be here,' he said at last, aware that the words sounded inadequate.

'Really glad,' added Fiona to emphasise his meaning.

But Aunt Isobel seemed instinctively to understand how they felt and led them and their cases out into the car park.

'You probably haven't met one of these before,' she remarked, pointing ahead at what Robert regarded as a most peculiar, eccentric-looking vehicle.

'A 2cv Citroen. Thirteen years old and still a willing workhorse. The best I've ever had.'

But by now Robert had put down his cases and was gazing in astonishment at the starting handle poking out from under the radiator.

'I've never seen one of those,' he gulped.

'Battery is a bit temperamental these days so I just give the old handle the odd swing and away she goes like a bird.'

Fiona smiled. One minute a workhorse, the next a bird. She must have an imagination of sorts . . .

'Benjamin calls her Bronco because she bucks about a bit on bad roads,' explained Aunt Isobel, carefully unlocking the doors as if she were opening the Royal Mint and the Crown Jewels had been inside. Robert wondered a little unkindly who on earth would ever dream of stealing a thing like that.

Admittedly, he thought, the paintwork looked in good order, the tyres seemed okay and inside the car everything was spotless, if somewhat spartan. He noted with interest a neat little 35mm camera tucked down beside her seat. After they had loaded in the luggage he got into the back seat to let Fiona see the scenery better, and he was startled to see what looked like the top third of an umbrella sticking out from the dashboard under a sign which read *'Ne fumez pas. Nicht rauchen.* No smoking.'

'Aunt Isobel, just what is that?' he asked, pointing.

'That,' she replied authoritatively, 'is the gear lever.'

'You're joking.'

Aunt Isobel jerked it into neutral, turned the ignition key and then got out and went to the front of the car, shouting out, 'This will be your job, Robert, in the future.'

He watched her bend down; her head bobbed up and down a couple of times, the car jerked in rhythm with her movements and then gave a convulsive shudder as the engine shook itself to life. Then the clattering began as she tucked the starter handle under her seat and pulled the door shut.

Aunt Isobel did something in a peremptory fashion with the umbrella handle and the Citroen moved forward with a grating sound. She turned sharply at the end of the row of parked cars and it heeled over with protesting sounds from the suspension system.

By now she had moved the umbrella handle again and the car was going at a steady 10 mph. Another gear change, the engine note became less protesting and soon they were out onto the Prestwick bypass heading north-east.

Robert watched fascinated as the speedometer gradually crept up to an indicated 55 mph.

Aunt Isobel saw him in the driving mirror. 'Bronco will do another ten miles an hour on a good day.'

Robert mumbled, 'I'm sure she will,' but inwardly wondered whether this was not already straining the poor vehicle.

Aunt Isobel drove with keen-eyed concentration, hands firmly on the wheel. Progress over the near 100-mile route, including the long open stretch over wild Fenwick Moor, was slow. And every time they had to stop Aunt Isobel had to go through a process called double de-clutching to get into first gear.

'Doesn't have any synchromesh on first,' she explained. 'It makes it more interesting – and more rewarding too.'

'Rewarding?' queried Robert.

'Yes, if you get it spot on there's not a sound to be heard.'

Fiona, turning in her seat, smiled at Robert, who knew what she was thinking. Why then all the weird grating sounds when first was engaged? But both were too polite to comment.

Anyway they had already discovered that Aunt Isobel enjoyed delivering what they were later to hear described as 'monologues'. On this occasion they took the form of interesting descriptions of historical associations with the passing countryside. She possessed an unnerving aptitude for apparently knowing what they were thinking, for in the middle of a ghoulish piece about a ghost who roamed Fenwick Moors she abruptly turned and looked first at Fiona and then Robert.

'Getting a free history lesson.' It was more of a statement than a question but Robert felt it deserved some comment.

'And it sure is interesting.'

'I believe you mean it.'

'Oh yes I do, Aunt Isobel.'

'Really he does,' put in Fiona, anxious that their aunt should not think he was pulling her leg. 'He'll read any old thing about Scotland. You've no idea the rubbish he had at home . . . ' Her voice tailed off. 'I didn't quite mean it like that.'

Aunt Isobel smiled. 'I know you didn't, Fiona.'

Robert remembered her tartan bonnet jammed into his reefer jacket pocket. He pulled it out. 'This is my lucky talisman,' he declared.

'It saved his life,' said Fiona.

'So you told me, my dear.' Her voice was soft, the gentle accent more marked.

Robert began to sense that perhaps she was more sympathetic than she at first appeared. 'I've got every single Scottish present you've ever given me,' he said.

'Have you now? That's a lovely thing to say.'

Another hour passed with Aunt Isobel beginning, almost tentatively for her, to ask them questions about the flight and their last months at home. Though tired they talked animatedly then became silent as they approached the 'Fair City of Perth'.

Over what Aunt Isobel described as the 'Gateway to the Highlands', it was a fine summer's day. Blue sky with a long strip of cumulus clouds billowed up on the horizon over the hills. Eagerly Robert looked out at the streets – gas stations, small shops, grey stone houses, and the sun sending slanting shadows over the pavements.

Fiona too was absorbing everything. The strangeness of it rather than the superficial similarities caught her eye first. It was different from what she had imagined. But when Aunt Isobel announced that she would take them down Tay Street so they could 'admire the bridges,' she gasped with delight. Tall trees lined the roadside: beyond, the river danced in the sunlight, an angler was casting for salmon and ahead Robert counted the nine arches of the Perth Bridge spanning the Tay.

Pointing to the bridge Aunt Isobel remarked: 'Over the years the levels of serious floods are marked on the bridge. I can still mind the three occasions between 1945 and 1952 when the Tay flooded the Inches.'

'So you have floods here,' exclaimed Robert.

'Not now, thanks to the Hydro. The dam up at Pitlochry more or less solved the problem of floods in the city.'

'And what are the Inches?' asked Fiona.

'The North Inch used to be a race course and in 1396 the great battle of the Clans was fought there.'

Robert leaned forward excitedly. 'I read all about it in *The Fair Maid of Perth* by Sir Walter Scott.'

'Did you now? You are a strange lad.'

Fiona explained. 'Robert will read anything, but anything about Scotland and especially Perth.'

'So you're really a budding historian.'

'Oh, I wouldn't say that,' replied Robert modestly. 'It's just that, well, ever since I was a child I've been sort of fascinated by anything to do with Scotland.'

Aunt Isobel swung the Citroen over with a violent twist of the wheel and a short time afterwards she drew up outside a solid-looking stone house. There was a wooden gate framed with yellow roses and a red gravel path leading up to the front door.

Gratefully Robert and Fiona stretched their legs as they stood on the pavement and studied their new home.

It was just about as different from their old home as it could be and Robert wondered about the future.

He had been so anxious to come and now he felt – homesick? He glanced at Fiona.

Their eyes met and he saw the uncertainty in hers and felt responsible for the decision to wrench them away from Jasper.

Robert felt Aunt Isobel eyeing them. 'Too much excitement in too little time.'

He nodded, grateful that she seemed to understand.

'Out with the cases,' she said brusquely and, opening the gate, marched up the path. 'I'll fetch you a cup of broth,' she called over her shoulder.

'She means well, Robert.'

'It sure makes me feel strange though.'

'I know. Me too.'

They reached the stone doorway and Fiona paused. Robert looked at her inquiringly as she put down her big case and gently touched the wall of the old house.

He dropped his own cases, feeling the warmth of the sun on his back, vaguely aware of the scent of the roses and then becoming conscious of the coolness of the house itself. Not a musty smell, just a smell of age and welcome. Yes, that was it. Fiona would be feeling the same as she now pressed the palm of her hand firmly against the stone, feeling the texture, sensing the mood of the house.

Finally she smiled at him. 'We're home, Mac.'

He grinned back at her. 'Good old Fiona. You always know.'

'Usually.'

They crossed the threshold and somewhere in the recesses of the old house a grandfather clock gave a single mellow chime.

'The house is welcoming us, Mac.'

In her own brusque way Aunt Isobel extended the welcome with a tall glass filled with sparkling amber liquid.

'Home-made cider from apples in the back garden,' she announced with a touch of pride. 'And a cup of soup to cheer you up.'

Robert felt it was odd to have soup on a summer's day but gratefully drank it. It was followed by thick slices of cold roast beef and salad with a heap of grated carrot on the edge of the plate. Robert grimaced. If there was one thing he didn't like it was grated carrot. As the meal progressed the pile of carrot gratings remained and Robert became aware that Aunt Isobel was regarding his plate with growing irritation.

Fiona was making signs to him to eat it.

'Raw carrot is very good for you,' announced Aunt Isobel.

'Yes,' he mumbled, feeling he had to say something.

'But you seem to be leaving yours. Is it not to your liking then? Not up to American standards.'

'Canadian,' he corrected her, not for the first time.

'American or Canadian, it's all the same to me, across the Atlantic, the land of beefburgers.' She almost spat the words out with disgust.

'It's just great,' he said.

'Really it is,' added Fiona to support him.

'So why are you leaving your carrot to the end?'

Robert thought desperately. 'When I eat Banana Dream Boat I always leave the ice-cream to the end because I like it so much.'

Aunt Isobel snorted, though he could see a gleam of amusement in her blue eyes. 'I can't abide politicians and that's a politician's answer if ever I heard one.'

Fiona looked upset. 'Robert's not like that, really he isn't. He's just being polite. Oh.' Her hand went to her mouth.

Aunt Isobel, who had just finished scraping the last morsel of food from her plate, laid down her knife and fork. 'In this house manners are important but,' and her face broke into a smile, 'not half so important as truth and honesty. I'll ask you to mind that in future.' She turned to Robert. 'There'll be no more raw carrot for you my lad.'

Aunt Isobel got to her feet, whisked away his plate, buried herself in the fridge and produced a dish of coloured ice-cream.

'This will be more to your liking I'm thinking.'

'Oh yes,' he breathed with delight.

Afterwards, when they had dried the dishes, Fiona came through to his room, where he was unpacking.

'You know what I think, Mac.'

'No.'

'I think Aunt Isobel is nervous.'

'Nervous?' he echoed.

'Yes, nervous of us. She's not had any children of her own and here we are sort of thrust upon her.'

He looked at her for a moment. 'Perhaps you're right. But heck she *is* a school teacher.'

He thought back to those first impressions as he entered the house and frowned in concentration. Something was niggling him but he could not think what it was.

Fiona took from him the shirt which he was about to bundle into one of the ill-fitting drawers in the old oak wardrobe, and carefully hung up his Matheson tartan kilt.

'What is it, Robert? Why so serious all of a sudden?'

He sat down on the edge of his bed. 'I think Aunt Isobel was worrying about something – after she had got into the house I mean.'

Fiona placed the shirt in the drawer.

'I still say she was nervous about having us.'

'But why? We're hardly aliens from outer space.'

'All the same . . . '

He stood up. 'I've got it. Remember the smell of the house?'

Fiona wrinkled her nose. 'The smell of an old house. But it was also a welcome smell.'

'I know that.' He was irritated. 'We both sense the same things. But as we passed the sitting-room – '

'I smelled pipe tobacco.'

'Recent pipe tobacco.'

'Yet,' said Fiona, 'Aunt Isobel stayed the night in Prestwick, she told us that in the car.'

'So someone was in this house recently – perhaps without her permission.'

Fiona looked at him, a serious expression on her elfin features: 'So now who's imagining things?'

Downstairs they could hear the sound of windows being flung open. Robert crossed the room and, standing at the door, recalled the *No smoking* sign in three languages in Bronco. Surely only a woman who felt strongly about smoking and the smell of tobacco would put such a sign in her car. She would hardly tolerate anyone smoking in her house . . .

There was a faint hissing sound. It must have lasted for half a minute. Then silence. Finally there drifted up to them the strong smell of lavender.

'That was Aunt Isobel using an aerosol,' Fiona said quietly.

'Yes, trying to mask the smell of tobacco.'

Fiona's green eyes gleamed. 'Now I ask myself, why should she be so fussed about a little tobacco smoke!'

Arisaig – a new home for Robert and Fiona

Chapter 8
PREMONITION

The sharp smell of the aerosol grew stronger as they made their way down the steep, narrow, curving staircase.

'No sound of Aunt Isobel,' whispered Fiona.

'Probably in the kitchen.'

'So we can explore then,' said Fiona, a tremor of excitement in her voice.

'Reckon so. And we start with the living-room.'

And start with the living-room they did. A large well-proportioned room, high ceilinged, with a fine marble fireplace, long narrow windows – wide open – in the old Scottish style, and on the walls old prints and photographs of Perth. Discreetly in the corner was a TV set, with a radio nearby, and over by the left of the fireplace in a lighted wall cabinet were two shelves of exquisitely painted enamel boxes.

'Oh, they're really beautiful,' she exclaimed. 'Just look, Robert.'

Fiona could not have chosen a more appropriate moment to comment for she had barely completed her sentence when Aunt Isobel came into the room.

'I'm glad you think so.'

'Oh yes.' Fiona, still peering through the glass, was growing ecstatic, 'They're just magic.'

'You appreciate beautiful things then,' more of a statement than a question but Fiona, in her element, responded to the remark.

'Art was my best subject at school.'

Robert, proud of his sister's accomplishment, added, 'She has got up a great portfolio.'

'A portfolio now.' Aunt Isobel sounded impressed. 'You shall have to let me see it. And soon.'

Robert liked the sound of 'And soon.' It suggested she meant what she had said and was not merely being polite. Friends back home had often expressed the same intention but never followed up their initial display of interest.

Fiona said eagerly, 'I'll show them to you.'

'That is something for me to look forward to. I am a photographer but I have the eye

29

of an artist.' Robert looked again at the frame photographs. 'Those yours?' When she nodded pleased assent he added. 'Why they're just top grade. Top grade, Aunt Isobel.'

Fiona, however, was now gazing into the cabinet. 'Some of these – the Easter egg ones – are modern.'

'Yes, a Bilston firm produces one to commemorate each year.'

'But the others, they look much older.'

Enthusiasm for her hobby was evident as Aunt Isobel replied, 'Oh yes, they are nearly all eighteenth-century South Staffordshire. And some of them are very valuable. In fact one or two of the finest examples are worth hundreds of pounds each.'

'Really,' exclaimed Fiona in awe.

'See that etui.'

'Etui?' asked Robert, not really interested in the subject and browsing through a pile of camera magazines.

'They were designed to hold a pencil, ivory slips, a penknife, a snuff spoon, a bodkin and scissors.'

'Quite useful,' commented Robert, looking at a comparative review of zoom lenses.

'Oh yes they were. This – you can see how it is delicately tapered at the bottom – was made around 1770 and the artist decorated it with lakeside and country scenes.'

'I love all that beautiful pink,' said Fiona, 'and the gold enamelling is awfully well done.'

'It is precisely that Bilston pink as it is called and the gold that make it worth so much money.'

Aunt Isobel opened the cabinet, lifting the etui with infinite care and held it in the afternoon light from the window so they could inspect it better.

After letting Fiona hold it she carefully replaced the etui in the centre of the second shelf and launched into one of her monologues about formulae for producing the enamels used centuries ego. As she talked on, Fiona in her mind was still savouring the cool translucent texture of the piece.

Robert, by now studying with interest an old print of the North Inch, asked, 'But why do you collect English enamel boxes? Why not good Scottish ones?'

Aunt Isobel laughed. 'I wish there were good Scottish ones.'

Robert walked towards her.

'Well, why did you not collect Scottish things?'

'You really are a Scot,' said Aunt Isobel sitting back in one of the armchairs flanking the fireplace.

Robert said stubbornly, 'I've always been a Scot. And now . . .' He stopped, wondering when he should tell Aunt Isobel about his quest. Not yet. It was too soon, he decided. Perhaps when he knew her better.

'My father, your grandfather Matheson, began collecting them before the war when he worked as an engraver in Staffordshire. I inherited the collection and have been adding to it – very modestly – ever since.'

'And that,' said Robert questioningly as he pointed at the etui, 'is the most valuable piece in your collection.'

She regarded him keenly for a moment. 'Yes. And I doubt I shall ever be able to afford anything as good again.'

He studied the flawless finish, wondering how much it was worth.

'Surely it should be locked away,' he said at last.

'There would be no point in having it then,' she remarked. 'It is beautiful and it gives me pleasure there.'

Feasting her eyes on it, Fiona had a strange feeling. It was as if time had moved on.

30

Morning sunshine was streaming through the south-facing windows. All trace of the aerosol perfume had gone.

And so too had the etui!

She was staring horrified at an empty space in the cabinet. She had to be dreaming she told herself. But it was all so vividly real . . .

Aunt Isobel's voice brought her abruptly back to the present. 'Fiona, what is it? Are you all right?'

Fiona rubbed her eyes and blinked. It must have been a trick of light. The etui, with its glowing rose pinks and golds, still stood there – testimony to a rare talent that had flourished nearly 200 years ago.

Slowly she looked round at Aunt Isobel and opened her mouth to try and explain what had happened. But what exactly had happened? Even she, used as she was to the occasional premonition, was uncertain . . .

'Well,' said her aunt, not unkindly.

The phone rang, cutting across the stillness in the gracious living-room with its windows open to the scents of the garden, and perhaps to dissipate the smell of tobacco smoke and aerosol perfume? Robert wondered about that as Aunt Isobel rose swiftly to her feet and walked into the hall. He glanced across at his sister.

'You saw something, Fiona?'

Fiona smiled ruefully. 'Yes.' She looked back at the cabinet but the etui was still there. So was it just a case of imagination?

Aunt Isobel's voice came clearly into the living-room from the hall where she was standing, phone in hand. 'My young nephew and niece from Alberta, you know Hugh's children, have just arrived so this afternoon wouldn't be suitable.

'Tomorrow? Eleven o'clock would suit fine.'

Silence for a moment.

'That seems a good idea, after all Steve will be in the same class as Robert when he goes to school next term.'

Another pause.

'No reason why Pete shouldn't go with them.'

A long pause this time.

'No I shall *not* forget. I shall write it in my diary this very moment.'

Robert and Fiona looked at each other, wondering who Steve and Pete were. Aunt Isobel went into the kitchen to return almost immediately with a huge diary in her hand.

'Mustn't forget to make a note for tomorrow,' she announced and proceeded to scribble something on one of the pages.

Robert wondered if it were polite to ask her what it was all about.

'Now you'll want to know all about Steve and Pete.' She looked at them. 'Now don't look so abashed. I always listened to father's telephone conversations. Mother's were too dull to be of any interest.'

Robert felt a bit shamefaced but said nothing. Fiona was on her best behaviour. 'Yes please.'

'Ena McLarnty is an –' she hesitated, '– acquaintance. To be exact, she works on behalf of the Relief of Famine Group. We are still collecting for the refugees. Poor creatures,' she shook her head sorrowfully. 'Such a disaster.'

'And Steve – who is he?' asked Fiona.

Aunt Isobel laughed gently. 'Bless you.' Then turning to Robert, 'And I suppose you want to know if there is a glamorous sister.'

Robert felt his face growing red. He scowled at his shoes and noted that they had not been cleaned for weeks. But that knowledge, which certainly should not have come as a surprise, did not help him. 'Well, er.'

Fiona looked impish. 'Go on, Robert, out with it. Of course you hope there is.'

Aunt Isobel was contrite. 'That was unfair of me. I'm sorry. There is no sister, glamorous or otherwise and for your sake I am very glad.'

Robert was both crestfallen and intrigued.

'But there are some very nice lasses in the next street and I am sure you will get to know them soon enough.'

'What's Steve like?'

Aunt Isobel closed her diary with a snap. 'A big lout of a lad with a head too big for his boots – more's the pity. But I've known worse in my day.'

'And Pete?' asked Robert.

'He's the one you've got to watch. I hear tell they call him the Weasel. Fourteen but already addicted to his computer. It's unnatural.'

Fiona looked puzzled. 'Well, why are we seeing them tomorrow?'

'Oh did I tell you then?'

Fiona answered, 'Well not exactly.'

Aunt Isobel replied matter of factly. 'But of course you were listening into my conversation.' Not waiting for a comment, she continued.

'You are bound to see them sometime, at school if not sooner. And more to the point they are Ena McLarnty's sons so it would be the height of bad manners for me not to agree when she suggested you all met tomorrow.' She looked at each of them in turn. 'Now does that answer your question?'

'Oh yes,' replied Fiona, nodding her head in case this strangely outspoken aunt should misunderstand.

But there loomed up in Robert's mind a question which it did not answer. Just what was so unnatural about being dead keen on a computer? Back in Jasper half the school were mad about computers. While he was out skiing or reading up about Scotland and the clans they were hunched up over their computers.

So just why had Aunt Isobel said he was the one they had to watch? And why was he called the Weasel?

Extract from Fiona's diary

I feel real pooped tonight. My head's all a buzz – so many different impressions shooting about. Saying goodbye to Jasper and all our friends. The long, long flight – it just seemed to go on for ever and ever – then the excitement when Mac and I saw Arran.

And then meeting Aunt Isobel – but I'll write about her properly in a moment. The crazy journey in that old as the hills wagon of hers. Bronco she calls it. Yeah and Bronco it is.

Then Arisaig – that's our new home. It felt like home too when I touched the stone of the outside walls. It's an old, old house – tiny bathroom and midget toilet halfway up the staircase on the bend. Bedrooms are OK. Mine's got a steep cam ceiling though and it slopes down almost to the floor on one side. But it faces right for painting and there's a bookcase with room for all my painting and ballet books – and Omar Khayam of course. He's the best of my poets. Gee, I'd sure like to know it all off by heart.

But now to Aunt Isobel. Here goes in my best literary style. Wait, I see I haven't even written down why I'm starting this diary. That's important really if you come to think of it. I mean just starting it out of the blue when I'm silly and stupid with tiredness and excitement.

Well Mac and I – we're starting a new life in a new country. I think I should put down my impressions of everything – and what goes on in my mind too. Because thoughts – and 'specially feelings – are dreadfully important.

So this is DAY 1 and now to Aunt Isobel at last:

Tall, angular, bony. If my English teacher back in Jasper had asked me to describe Aunt Isobel, these are the words I'd have used. And attractive too I suppose, especially to men. She's got a look about her. She has nice slim legs and her skirts are a bit short as if to say look at my legs.

Yes, when she was younger I imagine she must have been VERY attractive.

Her voice is Scottish, well I mean it would be. But it is soft and firm all at once and quite deep really when you listen to it carefully. She didn't kiss us or anything but put her arms round us and I know I felt welcome and – safe. Yes, safe as if I had come home. But then perhaps that is because Perth or at least Perthshire is our real home. After all this is where Robert and I were born.

I still think of us as Mathesons but Robert keeps reminding me we are really Kinlochys, a bit difficult that. Anyway Aunt Isobel is a Matheson and so is part of me.

I'm better at drawing things than describing them in words but Aunt Isobel would be difficult to draw properly because you feel there is more to her than you really see. Perhaps she is a mystery lady with a secret lover . . .

Oh dear, there's my imagination running away with me again. Miss Regan said I was 'prone' to doing that. I keep meaning to look up prone but I never have. Anyway I know what she meant and so I am – imaginative I mean. But I bet that there's a lot to Aunt Isobel and we'll just have to wait to find it out.

So do I call her romantic? I've never thought of aunts – I mean she must be oh close on 45 – as romantic. Or parents and yet when I think back Mummy and Daddy were romantic with each other. You could see it in their eyes and the way they'd hold hands sometimes when they thought no one was looking. But nearly 45 and romantic – I mean really.

The Weasel

Chapter 9
THE WEASEL

'**I** bet that's him,' exclaimed Robert grabbing Fiona by the arm.
They were walking towards Balhousie Castle, regimental headquarters and museum of the Black Watch (now the Royal Highland Regiment). The McLarntys lived not very far away and, as Aunt Isobel had got held up with some baking, Robert and Fiona had agreed to go on ahead. Both were curious about Steve and Pete and when they had learned that the castle was nearby Robert had been keen to see it.

'I believe you're right,' breathed Fiona, studying the skinny figure approaching.

The face was pinched and white: elongated dangling wrists stuck out from the end of his shirt cuffs: strapped to his narrow waist was a walkman recorder, headphones clamped over his ears. But it was his walk which was the oddest thing about him. He moved in a jerky, staccato way, like an automaton.

'Gee, he's weird all right,' said Robert.

The Weasel stopped and looked up at them with flat cold eyes. When he spoke his voice had a curiously metallic bite.

'So you're the big shots from Alberta.'

Robert felt uneasy. He shrugged. 'And you're the mighty micro boffin.'

The skeletal figure pursed his lips. If anything the eyes grew colder. 'Only dead stupid people talk to me like that.'

Robert didn't know whether to laugh or shiver. The Weasel was talking like a gangster in a second rate movie.

The sun came out from behind a cloud and a long skinny shadow sprung up behind the Weasel. He glared at them.

'I hate humans.'

Then he turned and the shadow preceded him along the pavement.

Robert and Fiona exchanged glances but said nothing.

They reached turreted Balhousie Castle, standing in its own wooded grounds. Robert stopped and stared at the centuries-old building, its shadow dappled by morning sunshine.

'Now that is a piece of history for you.'

Fiona replied, 'I'd like to paint that, Mac.'

'Yeah, it's top grade. Just top grade.'

Pete peered up at them through half-closed eyes. 'Are you two coming or not?'

But by now Robert had wandered halfway up the drive. Inexplicably there came into his mind the reason for him being in Scotland. With renewed urgency he thought of his Quest, of the search for his identity that lay ahead. Would it be a long search, would it go back over centuries into an unknown past? Would he need a lot of money to carry it out?

In this castle, perhaps in its museum, a mecca for thousands of people from all over the world, there lurked a clue to that past. Maybe one of his ancestors, a Kinlochy, had his name in the register of those who had fought with the Black Watch?

Fiona had joined him.

'The past – it could be locked in there, Mac.'

He nodded. They were so different and yet they had so much in common. He tried to imagine the desolation he would be feeling if there had been no Fiona: if he had been alone in the world after his parents had been killed. But he failed to do so and was glad . . .

Only the broken, pinched shadow with grotesquely stretched wrists that slid in front of them heralded the approach of the Weasel. Robert turned uneasily to be met with the same flat, hard gaze.

'I asked you if you were coming.'

Robert held back his irritation with difficulty. 'I've not set my eyes on a real castle before.'

The Weasel slitted his gaze. 'You're looking – searching for something.'

Fiona opened her mouth but Robert imperceptibly shook his head. However, the Weasel noticed all right. He noticed everything, Robert decided.

'So you are. Control will be interested.'

Fiona's green flecked eyes looked startled. 'Control. Who is control?'

But Pete was already walking away from them with short, jerky steps.

When he shoved open his gate and they met his elder brother, Robert was amazed at the difference between them. Whereas Pete was scrawny and twitchy in his movements, Steve was fleshy and lethargic. The contrast was startling.

Girls, Robert thought, would probably find him attractive. He had an animal look, like a well-fed cat. But as for Aunt Isobel's description of him being loutish, it was too early to tell.

The Weasel, who had replaced his headphones outside the castle, pulled them off. 'This is them,' and there was contempt in his metallic voice.

'Hi,' said Fiona, a trifle uncertainly.

Robert nodded, waiting for the other to speak.

Steve kept his hands in his jeans' pockets and slowly looked them over, lingering just a bit too long for Robert's liking on Fiona.

'Want some ice-cream?' Steve said at last in a lazy Scottish voice.

'Sure,' replied Robert.

'That would be really nice.'

But first there was a brief meeting with Mrs McLarnty, a prim, sharp-faced woman, who nevertheless made them welcome. Then there was the ice-cream, great coloured dollops of it on bright yellow plates in a bright yellow kitchen.

Pete had barely touched his ice-cream. 'I don't want to get fat,' he explained in a keyed-up voice. 'Too much eating is bad for you.'

Steve commented, 'You eat nothing.'

'And you gorge yourself.' The Weasel put down his spoon and stood up from the table. 'I'm going to talk to Control.'

This time Steve regarded his younger brother warily. 'You've something to tell him?'

Pete jerked his head towards Robert. 'You're dead right I have.' He picked his nose. 'And questions too.'

Now Steve looked worried. 'Questions. You're not going to . . . '

Pete interrupted him, 'That's my business Steve. Just leave it all to me.'

Robert, intrigued, pretended to be spooning up his ice-cream. As for Fiona, she smiled innocently at Steve though her eyes were speculative.

In the background the front doorbell rang and a little later they heard Aunt Isobel talking to Mrs McLarnty. 'I think a sale of work would be an excellent idea,' she was saying.

Steve helped himself to more ice-cream without offering them any. 'That's all those two do – yak, yak, yak, on and on about the starving millions in Ethiopia.'

'I feel really sorry for them,' said Fiona anxiously. 'And they're not the only people who look starved.'

'You mean that brother of mine.'

'Well, he hardly touched his ice-cream,' she said tentatively. 'And he does look sort of frazzled.'

'He hardly touches anything, scared he is of putting on weight. Every blasted night he's on those scales and then he writes down his weight and feeds it into C – ' he stopped, hesitated then said, 'into his computer.'

Listening, Robert thought that an odd thing to do. 'And what does the computer tell him?' he remarked with a laugh.

'What do you mean tell him? That's a dumb thing to say.'

Robert shrugged not wanting to start an argument. 'Oh, nothing.'

'Well be careful what you say round here. Everything goes into that computer. And I mean everything.'

Robert felt a strange sensation run down his spine. 'Everything?'

'More or less. He even talks to the damned thing. When I am trying to go to sleep there he is next door muttering away to it.' He kneaded his thumb for a few seconds. 'It's unnatural.' He lapsed into silence.

Outside they kicked a ball against the garage doors for a while and Fiona wandered round the garden looking at flowers.

Later Steve asked Robert, 'What do you think of the house?'

Robert was surprised at the question. 'Sure it's great, just great. Plenty of room for us all.'

'Anything special about it?'

'In what way?'

'Mother says she collects things.'

'Oh you mean the enamel boxes in the living-room.'

Steve looked interested. 'Yes that's right. Valuable are they?'

'Sure. There's one in the middle of them all, an etui or something that's worth hundreds of pounds.'

Fiona, who had just joined them, added, 'Aunt Isobel is dotty about it. So would I be if it was mine. It's really magic.'

Robert, caught up in the conversation, remarked, 'She doesn't even lock the cupboard.'

'I bet there are one or two of the sharper antique boys around who'd pay a lot of cash for it,' said Steve.

36

Fiona looked at Steve to see if she could read his expression. Robert was quiet, thinking about his own probable need for money for his search.

Back in Arisaig while waiting for Aunt Isobel to cook the potatoes for lunch, Robert went into the living-room, switched on the light in the cabinet and stood gazing at the etui. He felt hypnotised by it. There came unbidden into his mind Steve's words about the sharper antique boys who would pay a lot of cash for it.

Fiona came and stood by him. Her voice was low, insistent.

'Forget it, Mac.'

Robert shook his head, trying to put it out of his mind.

'I wish,' said Fiona, 'we had never mentioned it to them.'

'Me too.'

'I felt,' she stopped, 'I felt that there was something phoney.'

'Phoney?' he echoed.

'Oh,' she flapped her hands with exasperation. 'I can't put a finger on it. But all that talk about Control and computers and not eating.' She pushed a slender hand through her fair hair.

'It's as if he wanted to become a sort of shadow. Oh I don't know.' And she sat on the settee, chin in hand, gazing into space.

Robert took one last look at the etui and switched off the light. The glowing rose pink and gold were suddenly subdued.

'Lock it away. Lock it away.' Fiona repeated the words as if she were in a dream. 'It must be locked away.'

But Robert was now studying another of the prints of old Perth, this one of Balhousie Castle itself, and was hardly conscious of her words. And as for Aunt Isobel, she was immersed in cooking the lunch and never heard her.

So no one paid any attention to what Fiona was saying which, as events turned out, was extremely unfortunate . . .

It was Aunt Isobel who suggested he wear his kilt.

'Lunch will be a little late today. Why not change into your kilt. I've never seen you in it.'

'Gee, I don't know about that.'

'Oh go on Mac. You look terrific in it. Really you do.'

So with some grumbling Robert went upstairs and took out from the wardrobe the kilt in the red Matheson tartan. It was a handsome tartan. There was no doubt about that but as he looked at it he wished it had been the Kinlochy tartan, always supposing such a tartan existed.

Aunt Isobel eyed him critically for a moment then smiled one of those rare warm smiles which lit up her whole face. 'Aye you make a bonny figure, Robert – Matheson.'

Had there been the faintest pause in between the two names? He wondered but soon forgot all about it because of the good impression he had created on his aunt, and sister, who was now saying, 'I'd sure like to do a portrait of you in your kilt, Robert Matheson – you know the kind of thing, gazing out at the mountains. A claymore in your hand . . .'

During the afternoon they went for a walk round Perth, a city of contrasts that sparkled in the sunshine. Historic buildings dating back to the 1700s, ancient winding vennels, dark and hidden from the sun, modern bustling thoroughfares, cars nosing their way through one-way systems and, down by the bridges and the North Inch, the Tay itself flowing majestically by. Impressions jostled together in Robert's mind.

Everything was fresh and exciting and he was glad to share it with Fiona.

They were strolling down South Street, which was bustling with shoppers, when Fiona stopped and pointed across the road.

'Look at that,' she exclaimed.

'That' was a figure of a Highlander in the uniform of the Black Watch standing on a plinth in a niche in the front of the old Salutation Hotel. Shading his eyes against the afternoon sunlight he tried to make out the details of the Highlander figure which was in deep shadow. Then he noticed a second one on the other side of the door.

At that moment a youngish, fair-haired man, whose attention had obviously been caught by Fiona's Canadian accent, stopped.

'They're quite commanding figures, aren't they?'

'Yes,' said Fiona.

'There is another one in the front of Balhousie Castle as well as in Inverness.'

'I'll remember that,' said Robert, turning towards the man and taking in the green tweed jacket with leather patches on the elbows, faded cords and tinted glasses.

The man smiled warmly at Fiona who, Robert knew from experience, had an 'effect' on men of all ages. 'A nice effect,' their mother used to say, but an 'effect' all the same.

'It's the Salutation Hotel and it has stood there for centuries. In fact there are some interesting historical incidents attached to the building.'

'Oh,' exclaimed Fiona with interest.

Tweed Jacket warmed to his theme. 'You have heard of Bonnie Prince Charlie.'

'Sure,' said Robert. 'I've read all about him and the '45.'

'Well it was on 25 July of that very year that he landed at Moidart with seven followers.'

Robert could not resist airing his knowledge. 'The Seven Men of Moidart.'

The man regarded him keenly from behind his spectacles and Robert had the feeling that he was confirming something in his mind.

'So you do know your history. In September 1745 Prince Charles came to Perth and stayed in Room 12 of the Salutation Hotel.'

Robert was intrigued. 'I didn't know that.'

'Nor would you know that when he rode into Perth he had only one golden guinea in his pocket but when he left he had collected some five hundred pounds from the good citizens of the Fair City.'

Robert looked across at the Highlander figures. 'Where did you say the other one was?'

'Balhousie Castle. It's in Hay Street, about twenty minutes walk from here, near the Bell's Sports Centre.'

'Gee thanks. I know the castle.'

'It was sweet of you to tell us all about it,' added Fiona.

'Not at all, it was my pleasure, Miss – ' he paused.

'Fiona Matheson, and this is my brother, Robert.'

Unexpectedly Tweed Jacket put out his hand and formally shook hands with each of them. 'I shall remember your names,' he said in a distinct voice studying each in turn as though mentally photographing them. 'A fine tartan that, the Matheson,' he said indicating Robert's kilt. Then before either had a chance to ask his name he had turned and walked off in the direction of the Tay.

'That was real nice of him.'

'Yes, he did go out of his way to be helpful,' remarked Robert. 'A bit strange all the same.'

But by now Fiona was halfway across the road and a second later was standing looking up at the Highlander figures. 'There's nothing in Jasper like these,' she said.

Robert grinned. 'Hardly.'

In fact, there was hardly anything at all in Jasper like Perth, he thought as they turned down into Tay Street and started to walk past the various municipal offices. As he did so he remembered that according to a map of the town George Inn Lane should be just a few yards ahead.

'The District Registrar's Office for births, deaths and marriages is somewhere about here,' he remarked trying to sound casual.

But he didn't fool Fiona. 'You just happened to think about it I suppose.'

He grinned back at her. 'Come on, we could learn who we really are.'

Fiona wrinkled her forehead. 'But Mac I know who I am. I don't think I really want to be someone else.'

Robert began to feel annoyed until he recalled that over the last few months there had been moments when he had wondered if he wanted to be anyone else but Robert Matheson. So with that thought in mind he said sympathetically. 'All right, Fiona, but at least come to the offices with me.'

'Of course, Mac.'

Seconds later they reached the old sandstone church and then turned left into George Inn Lane. A hundred yards on and there on their left was the Registrar's Office and, in the same building, Perthshire Tourist Office. But beside the door there was a notice which dismayed Robert. It closed daily at 4.30 p.m. and looking at his watch he saw it was already 4.28 p.m.

'Hell, I hope it hasn't shut.' And he raced ahead through the door, Fiona trailing doubtfully behind.

The office was on the left. He went through, all thoughts of Fiona forgotten. Ahead of him were two doors marked *Enquiries*. He took the one on the left.

At first he thought the office was deserted. Behind the counter, there were typewriters, files, desks and chairs. But no one to be seen.

'Hello,' he called out. 'Anyone around?'

'Coming.' And an attractive girl in her twenties, slim, auburn-haired, in a summer frock came from the right of the counter ahead of him. 'We're about to close,' she told him.

Robert's shoulders slumped. 'Gee, I had hoped that you might be able to help me.'

Maybe it was the combination of the Canadian accent and the kilt, or the forlorn look on his features, for she took pity on him.

'Well as long as it's not too complicated.'

Robert took a deep breath before sitting down in front of the counter. Her brown eyes regarded him sympathetically and with a shock he realised that this would be the first time he had told anyone about his search to discover his real identity. He had thought about it often enough, rehearsed conversations in his mind, but never actually told anyone.

'I was adopted,' he began.

'In this country?' she asked. 'Because we have a special section for adoption.'

'Er . . . I don't know. Least I guess I was adopted in Canada.'

'That makes it more awkward.' Then she smiled cheerfully. 'But you will know your real name?'

Robert hesitated for a fraction of a second. Now it had to be out in the open. 'Kinlochy.'

She looked thoughtful. 'Kinlochy?'

'Yes. Is there something wrong?'

'No, it was just that I thought I heard one of my colleagues mention that name some time ago.' She leaned across the counter. 'You're sure you've not been here before.'

'Of course I'm sure. I only arrived here from Canada yesterday morning.'

'Oh well, it must have been a similar name then.'

'Yes,' he remarked trying to be helpful.

39

She wrote it down. 'And your date of birth.'

'The fifteenth of February nineteen – ' And so it went on, place of birth, etc.

She walked away and he could hear her turning pages. At last she came back, a huge file in her hands. 'You are sure about the date and place of birth.'

'Yes. Well, at least I think I am. I mean I'm certain about my birthday.'

'But not your place of birth.' She picked up another file and read aloud. 'In certain circumstances some adoptions granted abroad can be recorded in the adopted children's register.'

He perked up at hearing this.

'What it means, I'm afraid, is that you'll have to go to the Central Registrar's Office in Edinburgh. Here's a leaflet explaining everything to you,' and she handed him six flimsy blue sheets covered with closely set text. 'And I'm afraid I have to ask you for one pound and sixty pence for carrying out an unsuccessful search.' She paused and looked at him. 'I do hope you are successful. And good luck to you, Mr Kinlochy.'

Chapter 10
BREAK-IN

Steve looked fleshy – and dangerous

Outside standing on the pavement Robert felt bitterly disappointed. When he had first seen the building he had thought – Now I am going to learn something important about myself.

'Mac, cheer up. It's not the end of the world.'

'Sure, it's my second day here. I shouldn't expect miracles.'

'And anyway Edinburgh is only down the road, isn't it?'

'I reckon so, Fiona. And as you say we've only just arrived.'

He looked across onto Tay Street. There he was again. The fair-haired man in the tweed jacket and tinted sunglasses.

'Well, that sure is a coincidence,' he remarked. 'There's that guy who told us about the Salutation Hotel.'

Fiona looked across the road. 'Where?'

'Over there,' he said pointing to the far pavement.

'I don't see him.'

'No, he's lost behind those cars.'

'But are you sure, Robert, that it was him?'

Robert rubbed his chin. 'Not one hundred per cent sure.'

'Then you're probably imagining it.'

So it was in a more thoughtful frame of mind that they wandered back to Arisaig and to their second Scottish high tea in the big, old-fashioned kitchen. Robert ran his finger along the top of the pine table, marked and mellow with age. 'How old is it?'

Aunt Isobel finished the last of her bacon and eggs and carefully placed her knife and fork side by side on the plate – all part of a ritual.

'Old as the house I should think.'

Fiona looked across at her. 'And you said the house was built back in . . . ' she wrinkled her forehead.

'Eighteen fifty-four,' prompted Robert.

'You'll be an historian yet,' remarked Aunt Isobel. 'It's interesting to think that this house has been in the family since 1865.'

Robert grinned cheekily. 'And that camera you were playing with this morning. It looked about as ancient as the house.'

'Don't be so superior about old cameras young man. That Robot was made in 1935. Ahead of its time it was.'

'How?'

'It is a perfect candid shot camera. Motor drive, square format, forty-eight shots per thirty-six spool, and colour coded distance and stop markings to save you the bother of focussing.' She paused. 'But I mustn't bore you with all this.'

'No, go on.' Robert leaned across the table. 'It interests me.'

So while Fiona discreetly helped herself to a slice of home-made Madeira cake, Aunt Isobel settled back in her chair and began to talk of her hobby with mounting enthusiasm. 'Of course, Robert, the great advantage of that little Robot is in its viewfinder.'

'How come?'

'It swivels round to one side so unless someone is studying what you are doing very carefully you can take a photo of that person without them knowing.'

'Gee, that is ingenious.'

'And remember that was standard in 1935. Add to it a crisp f2.8 Carl Zeiss lens and you have a useful if rather heavy little camera.' Her eyes lit up. 'But you should see my early Contax with its f2 Sonar. You know the Russians copied that over twenty years later. Shows how good a design it was.'

'How many cameras do you have?'

'Not a great number.' But there was pride in her voice when she added, 'Seventy-five altogether.'

Fiona nearly choked on her cake and even Robert was impressed. 'For a woman that sure is something.'

'What on earth do you mean by a phrase like that?' Aunt Isobel was indignant. 'I didn't expect to have a male chauvinist under my roof.'

'Gee, I'm sorry. I didn't mean it like that.'

'And so you should be. Let me tell you, young man, that I have exhibited on several notable occasions.'

'I didn't reckon you were – well good as that. Have you had any published – in the papers I mean.'

'As a matter of fact I have.' And she mentioned a number of publications. Then abruptly she stopped.

'Now that was quite unforgivable of me. Boasting. A most annoying trait. And it was all thanks to you, Robert.'

He smiled. 'We'll forgive you Aunt Isobel.'

Fiona, recalling how her first serious interest in painting began when she won a prize for a watercolour of Pyramid Lake at the age of nine, asked. 'What made you interested in photographs in the first place?'

'That was all due to Hugh – your father. It was his tenth birthday and he had been given a second-hand Voigtlander – I remember it had an f3.5 Color Skopa lens and he asked me how it worked. Well I did not know a take-up spool from a rangefinder but I would not have admitted that to him.'

Fiona smiled to herself knowing that feeling well, especially when Robert had asked her questions which she really could not answer.

'Anyway,' continued Aunt Isobel, 'I read up all about cameras and became fascinated by them. I used to borrow Hugh's for a time. It was rather naughty of me.'

'Why?' asked Fiona.

Aunt Isobel leaned forward as if she were about to impart a secret. 'You see Hugh took months to finish a film so I used to wind back his film and put my own in and then when I had completed it I replaced his and he never knew.'

'Never?' asked Robert astonished.

'No. Not once. I did it for a whole year and then my parents gave me a Ross Ensign – oh it had a beautiful lens, f3.5 Ross Ypress, 16 on and a focal length of I think it was 80mm or more, just right for portraits you know.' Her whole face lit up and Fiona could just imagine how she must have looked at her age.

'I used to take portraits of a certain young man. They were quite good.' She stopped and was silent for a moment, lost in memories.

'Then I decided I had to do my own processing so I saved up for a second-hand enlarger – a rickety old thing it was – and I have been doing my own printing ever since.'

'Colour too?' asked Robert.

'Good heavens, yes! I wouldn't trust my work to anyone else.' She stood. 'But that's enough for now. And what are you going to do tonight?'

'Read,' Robert replied promptly. 'You know that book in the living-room bookcase, the one by Sir James Balfour Paul?'

'Oh yes, *Scottish Family History*.'

'That's the one. Can I borrow it tonight?'

'Of course. You may read any of my books, but always make sure you put them back exactly where they came from and never dog-ear the pages.'

'That's something,' replied Robert emphatically, 'that we would never do.'

Now Fiona was thinking of something else. 'Tell me, Aunt Isobel, why is the bathroom so small.'

'And the toilet as well. I can only just get in and . . .' his voice tailed off in sudden embarrassment. But it was the smallest he had ever seen, tucked away under the staircase, a doll's-size basin only inches away from the wooden lavatory seat and a stained glass window looking onto the long back garden.

'It's quite simple really. They just didn't have bathrooms and toilets in those days.'

'Oh,' exclaimed Fiona, looking very fastidious all of a sudden. 'How uncomfortable for them.'

Aunt Isobel laughed. It was such a clear happy laugh that they both found themselves laughing till the tears came into their eyes and a crumb of Madeira cake stuck in Fiona's throat and she started choking.

'You're a delightful child,' said Aunt Isobel.

And Fiona, still half choking, never bothered to remind her that, like Robert, she was not a child.

Robert wiped his eyes. 'What were they then?'

'Well, the toilet was originally a tiny cupboard and the bathroom was the boxroom. That's why it has no window.'

In the hall the mahogany grandfather clock, made, said Aunt Isobel, by a George Findley of Arbroath in the early 1800s, chimed the half hour.

'Half past six,' exclaimed Aunt Isobel. 'Come on now, we've gossiped enough for one night.'

But she had hardly started running the hot water for the dishes than the phone rang and this time she carefully closed the door behind her.

'That's odd,' remarked Robert, dish cloth reluctantly in his hands, 'she doesn't normally do that.'

'Ah, a mysterious stranger.'

'Don't talk nonsense. It wouldn't be a mysterious stranger if she expected a call from him.'

The kitchen door opened. 'That is a nuisance. Ena McLarnty has just got the collection boxes for the Famine Relief Fund and wants me to pick up mine.'

'I'll come with you,' volunteered Fiona.

'That would be an excellent idea. And what about you, Robert?'

'Thanks all the same, but I think I'll stay in and read *Scottish Family History*.'

Later, thumbing through the index at the back of the book he could find no reference to a Kinlochy. Disappointed, he went and stood opposite the lighted cabinet and studied the etui, trying to analyse its fascination for him: was it its value, its glowing colours, its elegant shape, or just its age?

'Just off now,' called Aunt Isobel from the hall.

Robert put down his book and took one last look at the etui.

'Think I'll take a walk myself into the town.'

'Oh,' said Fiona entering the room, 'I thought you were going to swot up Scottish families.'

'I changed my mind.'

'Well put off the cabinet light then.'

He switched it off and quickly left the room.

Outside, walking down the path towards the wrought-iron gate, he remarked, 'I'll come as far as Balhousie Castle with you.'

And so the three of them set off together in the soft evening air, but not before Aunt Isobel had paused to pull out a weed. 'This Shepherd's Purse would smother the borders if it got half a chance.'

They turned the corner at the end of the road and were walking in the direction of the castle when Robert glanced down the narrow walled path that ran behind Arisaig's back garden. It was in deep shadow but he thought he had seen something move, immediately below the wall.

He turned to Aunt Isobel. 'I think I'll go down to the North Inch first.'

Aunt Isobel looked surprised. 'Oh well, if you wish, but don't be late.'

He grinned a quick farewell and set off purposefully down the path, peering ahead. But there was no one in sight. Drawing level with the garden gate he stopped, put his hand on the latch and flung it open. The long deep garden, with its clump of apple trees and the birches, aspens and willows running down one side barely stirring in the breeze, was quiet and peaceful. He stood motionless, waiting, watching for a sign of someone – perhaps even an animal, a nocturnal tom cat on the prowl . . . But nothing. Finally, disappointed he closed the gate behind him.

*****

Robert opened the front door. 'I'm back,' he shouted.

Fiona ran into the hall. 'Where have you been all this time for heaven's sake,' she asked.

'What do you mean?' he asked in a puzzled tone.

Aunt Isobel appeared. 'Something very strange has happened when we were out. Something very strange indeed.'

Robert looked at his aunt. 'Oh.'

'Come upstairs,' was all she said.

The door of his bedroom was open: it was in chaos, bedclothes strewn on the floor, drawers open, clothes hanging out everywhere.

Robert was silent. It looked just as if a tornado had whipped through the room. 'And the rest of the rooms?'

'That is what is so peculiar, Robert,' replied his aunt. 'They are untouched. So I wonder what exactly they were looking for?'

Fiona caught her breath but said nothing: he had sworn her to secrecy.

Aunt Isobel regarded him sternly. 'I think *we* had better tidy it up.' She paused ominously. 'And see if they have missed anything.'

Fiona glanced at him. He barely raised an eyebrow in acknowledgement.

It took half an hour to restore some semblance of order to his bedroom.

Fiona stood up from folding away a heavy knitted sweater, and frowned. 'Why didn't you phone for the police?'

'Or were you waiting till I had returned?'

Aunt Isobel looked even more grave. She seemed to be pondering the question. 'I am not quite sure whether I will.'

'But surely,' began Robert.

'Surely nothing,' retorted his aunt. 'We have to get to the bottom of this. Not the police.'

Fiona was a little unsure of her choice of words. 'A postmortem at this time of night?' she asked.

Aunt Isobel glanced at her watch and relented. 'We'll discuss it tomorrow morning.'

Fiona was relieved. 'How did someone get into the house? I mean you locked the door when we left.'

Aunt Isobel looked disconcerted. 'Perhaps it was the back kitchen window. I tend to leave it open sometimes.'

'Yes I noticed that,' put in Robert a little too hastily.

'Very observant of you, Robert,' Aunt Isobel remarked quietly and then bade them both goodnight.

Extract from Fiona's diary

This has been the oddest of days. I mean to say Weasel is the oddest thing I've met. Really weird he is – like some robot from TV. Steve is like a well-fed cat. He's physical all right.

There is something odd about the Registrar's records. No record of Mac or me. We don't seem to exist – not here anyway. It made me feel a bit creepy as though we were ghosts from the past.

Then there was the rumpus in Mac's room. You'd have thought a tornado or something had gone through it. Who could have got in and why? He must have been looking for something. Mac reckons it was the napkin rings – anyway he's hidden them in an ancient box camera Aunt Isobel had shown him. But I think it was the paperweight and it's safe in my room. Well it better be because I've stuck it up the chimney and no one would look there.

Can't think why Aunt Isobel doesn't fetch the police along. Unless she's got something to hide – like why she keeps the kitchen window open on the sneck. I mean that sure is a crazy sort of thing to do.

I really hope we don't have any more days like this.

*****

She was not certain what woke her: the single chime of the mahogany grandfather clock or the sound of footsteps on the wooden hall floor. She listened and thought she heard a creak on the stairs or, was that her imagination? Another creak. Then silence.

Fiona turned on her back, now wide awake. Yet another creak. That was odd. She had already discovered that the fifth and twelfth stairs creaked badly but she could not remember another stair that creaked. The wind sighed outside and now it seemed that the old house was full of creaks and groans and little subterranean sounds, unidentifiable but somehow part of the fabric of Arisaig.

It was almost as if the house talked to itself, she decided. Perhaps Aunt Isobel or Robert had got up for something, though that seemed unlikely. So maybe after all it was just the old house making noises to itself. And with that thought in her mind she fell asleep.

But next morning the memory of those sounds was to come vividly back to her.

The knocking on her door and the insistent 'Are you awake yet?' uttered in Aunt Isobel's most commanding tones made her sit up.

She stretched out her arms. 'Yes.' She looked sleepily at her watch. Only 8.15 a.m. 'What is it?'

'Please come downstairs. Something terrible has happened.'

A moment later as she clambered out of bed she heard her aunt knocking on Robert's door.

She pulled on her dressing-gown and nearly bumped into Robert as he came out of his room.

'I wonder what on earth it can be,' she said.

'Can't think – not at this hour of the morning.'

They half ran down the stairs, Fiona behind Robert. Two creaks of a stair in quick succession then as they neared the bottom two more creaks . . .

Aunt Isobel was standing in the living-room, anguish written all over her face, looking at the lighted cupboard. 'I just cannot believe it,' she was saying. 'It cannot be true.'

Fiona felt a terrible sense of dread. She knew without looking what she would see. She dare not even glance at Robert.

With an effort Aunt Isobel pulled herself together. 'The etui – it has gone.'

Then Fiona and Robert looked into the cabinet. The empty space in the centre of the second shelf seemed to shriek out at them.

Aunt Isobel was pale. 'You know what this means.'

Robert nodded heavily. 'Police. We'll just have to call them in.'

46

Chapter 11
UNDER SUSPICION

Sergeant Wallace Ochilston's expression was menacing

Sergeant Wallace Ochilston was a well-built man in his mid-forties wearing a belted raincoat and dark grey trousers. His expression as he greeted Aunt Isobel at the front door was genial and for a few minutes they discussed the coming Famine Relief Flag Day. But when Robert and Fiona were introduced to him Robert noticed the shrewd assessing look in his eyes common to policemen all over the world.

'From Canada you are. Well, and how are you liking it in our fair city?'

Aunt Isobel, for some unknown reason, seemed anxious to answer for them almost as if they would say something out of turn.

'This is only their third morning here, Sergeant Ochilston.'

'And you've hardly arrived and there's a break-in,' he said, following Aunt Isobel into the living-room. 'Last night it was, you were saying over the phone, Miss Matheson.'

'That's right. We had gone for a walk and – '

Sergeant Ochilston interrupted. 'But you reported it only half an hour ago. At nine o'clock this morning.'

'That is so, but last night we – that is to say I, did not know that the etui had been taken.'

He brought out his notebook and a dark blue biro. 'Which suggests that last night you had no intention of reporting the incident.'

Aunt Isobel looked worried. She hesitated before replying.

'No. That is so.'

'Do you mind telling me why?'

'It seemed so unnecessary. Nothing had been taken.'

'So you thought.'

'Yes.'

'What exactly had happened?'

'My room had been burgled.'

'Your room, Robert?'

'Yes.'

'And no one else's?'

'That is correct, Sergeant Ochilston,' said Aunt Isobel anxiously.

The sergeant put down his notebook and regarded each of them in turn. 'Verra strange.'

Fiona, who had been watching wide-eyed, obviously felt she had to say something. 'It was a terrible mess, a real tip.'

He smiled. 'But your room?'

'Oh no, it was fine. Not a thing touched.'

'How do you know that?'

Fiona looked taken aback. 'Well I don't exactly know, but I'm sure all the same. You see there wasn't anything in *my* room.'

Her remark was followed by a small silence. Both the policeman and Aunt Isobel studied Robert thoughtfully.

'I see,' he said at last. 'But there was something in Robert's room.'

Fiona's eyes grew larger. '*No*, oh no. I didn't mean that.'

'And what have you to say, Robert?'

Thinking of how he had hidden everything, Robert felt his face grow red. 'There was nothing in my room. Just clothes and bits and pieces.'

'Verra strange. Your second day here and for no reason whatsoever the house is broken into and your room only is turned upside down.' He tapped the biro against his teeth. 'I'm finding that hard to swallow.'

'Perhaps that was just to mislead us,' said Aunt Isobel desperately.

'Mislead you, in what way?'

'Take our attention away from the etui,' suggested Robert.

'The etui?'

'Yes, I described it over the phone if you recall,' said Aunt Isobel.

'Aye, so you did,' remarked the sergeant in a conversational way.

But he did not deceive Robert. The sergeant had known perfectly well what the etui was but he had wanted, for some secret reason, to ask Robert to describe it. So was he a suspect? And why?

The sergeant wandered over to the cabinet. 'So this was the scene of the crime?'

'Yes. It occupied the empty space in the centre.'

He opened the cabinet and carefully took out a small blue enamelled box made in Bilston at the turn of the century.

'A bonny wee piece this,' he remarked, taking it to the light of the window.

Aunt Isobel could not resist the temptation to launch into one of her monologues on English enamel trinkets. Robert, studying him, could not decide whether he was absorbing what she said or was quietly analysing his own thoughts on the matter.

'Verra interesting,' he remarked at length.

'Thank you, Sergeant Ochilston,' replied their aunt.

He wheeled round on them. 'And the etui, you are saying it was taken last night?'

'Well of course,' said Aunt Isobel. 'When else?'

'When indeed?' He studied them keenly. 'Not later, like early this morning for instance.'

Robert heard Fiona draw in her breath and saw her eyes growing wider. So perhaps she had heard the footsteps on the stairs. And what then was her interpretation of them? Did she think he had stolen it?

'Yes, Fiona?' said the policeman.

'Nothing. I was just – ' her voice tailed off and she looked so miserable that he smiled at her.

'Not to worry lass, the truth will out in the end.'

'Yes I – I suppose so.'

'No supposing about it,' he retorted emphatically. He turned to Aunt Isobel. 'You explained earlier that you were all out yesterday evening.'

'Yes. We were off to the McLarntys.'

'All three of you?'

She hesitated. 'We set out together.'

'But,' interrupted the sergeant, 'you didn't all arrive together?'

'No. That is to say . . .' She paused.

Robert felt he had to say something. 'I decided to go on to the North Inch.'

'When was that?'

'Just a short time after we left Arisaig.'

'Oh and why was that, Robert?'

'I thought I saw someone down the lane behind the house.'

Aunt Isobel looked at him sharply. 'I didn't know that.'

'No. I didn't think there was any point in mentioning it.'

Sergeant Wallace Ochilston came and towered over him.

'A sudden decision was it then?'

'Yes.'

'On the spur of the moment, as you might say.'

'Well I did see someone,' Robert replied defensively.

'Ah, so you did see someone.'

'Well, I mean I thought I did.'

The policeman put down his notebook with an air of resignation. 'Now let's get this clear. You either saw someone or you didn't.'

'No it wasn't quite like that. I thought – '

'Ah, you thought.'

'Yes.'

'And what or who did you find?'

'As it turned out – nothing.'

Sergeant Ochilston raised his eyebrows in mock surprise.

Robert felt himself becoming desperate. It sounded all wrong in this question and answer, cat and mouse way of talking.

'I walked down the lane – quickly.'

'Why?'

'Because I wanted to catch whoever – or whatever – I thought I'd seen.'

'Good. Go on.'

'When I arrived at the back gate the lane was empty.' He looked across at Fiona and Aunt Isobel sitting opposite each other, both listening keenly to what he was saying. 'So I tried the gate very carefully.'

'It's not kept locked.'

'No,' said Aunt Isobel very quickly. 'I have never bothered to lock it.'

'No real reason to, I suppose. And what next, Robert?'

Robert closed his eyes in concentration. 'I opened the gate and looked inside the garden.'

'Inside the garden?'

'Yes,' he replied a little bewildered.

'And not behind the gate.'

'I – I never thought of that.'

'I see.' He clicked his biro against his teeth. 'And you saw – '

'Nothing at all. The garden was empty.'

And so the interview continued. Where had he gone? Down to the North Inch. What had he done? Walked by the river for a while. Seen anyone in particular? Not really. Children playing about. Young couples arm in arm. That sort of thing.

Then he had examined Robert's room, opened a few drawers, peered at his shelf of books on Scottish history, made a few appropriate comments and clumped back downstairs again – the squeak more pronounced than ever on the fifth and twelfth stairs.

The sergeant paused in the hallway and the grandfather clock, seeming to take the cue from him, began its deep mellow chime. They stood listening to it till the eleventh strike had chimed.

'Isn't it lovely?' exclaimed Fiona. 'Over 160 years old and still chiming away.'

'Aye, it is that,' replied the sergeant thoughtfully and, without changing the tone of his voice or expression on his face, looked across at the three of them standing at the foot of the stairs and asked, 'Of course you've no idea how he got in?'

Robert and Fiona looked at their aunt. She appeared worried again. 'No one else but me has a key.'

The sergeant was elaborately casual. 'Not even Robert or Fiona here.'

'No.' Aunt Isobel was emphatic. 'Not a soul.'

'And speaking hypothetically of course, Robert's room could not have been ransacked before you all left the house.'

Robert felt indignant. But it was Fiona who spoke out.

'That's a mean thing to suggest.'

'I'm not suggesting anything. Just making sure. That's all.'

He looked hard at Robert. 'Well my lad, what have you to say about that?'

'I did remain in the house a little longer than Aunt Isobel or Fiona. But I was in the living-room all the time.'

'Sergeant Ochilston, I think your insinuations are most unfair.'

'Are you saying, Miss Matheson, that at no time after supper Robert had time to go up to his room and create the havoc that you described.'

Fiona, playing with a strand of hair, said. 'None of us could have done all that just before we went out. It would have been impossible.'

Sergeant Ochilston nodded. 'Aye, from the state you said the room was in that makes sense, lass.'

'And,' interrupted Robert, thinking back to the previous evening, 'I couldn't have risked doing it after supper in case Fiona came in.'

'No, neither you could,' said Fiona giving her hair another tug as if to emphasise her remark.

'So we are no further on about how the burglar got into the house?'

In that second Robert remembered looking down the garden and seeing the back window slightly open. In fact he got the impression that Aunt Isobel kept it open permanently. He was just about to say so when Aunt Isobel remarked. 'Of course it's always possible that I had left a window open. It was a warm evening and I was going out only for a short time.'

'You would not like to be more definite.'

Aunt Isobel was emphatic. 'No. I would not.'

And with that the sergeant had to be satisfied, though as he said an ironic goodbye at the front door he contrived to leave Robert with the feeling that he was far from satisfied.

In fact, he had taken only a few heavy steps down the front path when he stopped, turned and said, 'Would you like me to send our security expert round and he can check all the windows and perhaps suggest window locks and Allen keys?'

50

Robert was surprised to see Aunt Isobel look upset at the suggestion. 'Oh, I don't think that would be necessary. We don't live in Fort Knox.'

'But consider the peace of mind you would have, Miss Matheson. No one would be able to enter your house without breaking a window.'

'Definitely not,' she said in an agitated manner. 'What I mean,' she went on as the sergeant's expression grew curious, 'is that – '

Fiona, sensing her embarrassment though unable to understand it, put in quickly, 'Aunt Isobel might lock herself out one day.'

The sergeant laughed, as if the idea were preposterous. Robert smiled to himself and Aunt Isobel looked both relieved and a little irritated at the suggestion.

'I'm sure we can consider your suggestion some other time.'

'That could prove too late, but if that is your decision, Miss Matheson.'

And with that warning hanging ominously in the air Sergeant Ochilston turned and walked heavily away down the path. He looked over his shoulder at the gate and shouted, 'Or at least get yourself a dog.'

For the rest of the day a feeling of gloom hung over everything. Time dragged for both Robert and Fiona who, as if by silent agreement, refrained from mentioning the subject of the missing etui. Aunt Isobel devoted the afternoon to 'doing the garden' and photographing a velvety scarlet rose named – inappropriately in her view – Chorus Girl which she had planted the previous autumn.

After supper Ena McLarnty came on the phone. 'I hear you have been done,' she announced after Robert had answered. He was a little taken aback.

'Done. What do you mean Mrs McLarnty?'

She sounded impatient. 'Broken into, of course. Now run and fetch Miss Matheson.'

He went out into the front garden where she was cutting some apricot coloured roses for the living-room.

Absorbed in her task her face was relaxed and she looked at peace with the world.

'Yes, Robert,' she said straightening up.

'It's Mrs McLarnty. She wants to talk to you about the – the burglary.'

Instantly he felt sorry for his aunt. Her face fell and she looked harassed. 'Damn the woman,' she exclaimed and, clutching a bunch of Serenade roses, she hurried into the house. Robert experienced a sense of guilt as he stood alone in the garden. He had brought all this upon Aunt Isobel. Had he and Fiona remained in Canada none of it would have happened.

He felt sorry also for himself. No trace of his birth certificate. Did that mean that no Kinlochy existed, that he was really someone else? A McLarnty – heaven forbid. And yet something told him that he and Fiona were Kinlochys and that their heritage lay buried deep in the heart of the Scottish Highlands. If only he could see the name printed somewhere.

Robert wandered back into the living-room to join Fiona sitting next to the window sketching the garden in the gathering dusk.

'Hey, that's not bad,' he exclaimed.

'It takes my mind off other things,' she said quietly.

He did not reply but pulled the already crumpled ancestry leaflet out of his pocket and sat down once again to study it. He was still reading when Aunt Isobel entered the room but she was too angry to notice the blue sheets in his hand.

'That woman is nothing but a busybody.' She strode across the room and glared out of the window. 'It's none of her business.'

'But who told her?' asked Robert.

'That useless lout of hers.'

'Steve,' said Robert with interest. 'I wonder how he knew about it?' But Aunt Isobel said nothing and occupied herself arranging the roses in a vase.

Extract from Fiona's diary

There I was last night – yes, only last night – writing about yesterday being such a horrid day and hoping there would be no more like it.

Today's been a nightmare. When I first saw that etui I knew something grizzly was going to happen.

But Robert – surely he's got more sense. Well I mean I know he has even if he is all crazed up about who he is and where he came from. So he needs money – now that is, because we do have money but it's in the bank and Aunt Isobel is responsible for it.

Mac acted peculiar – almost as if he were hiding something. I have the feeling he knows – knows what? Why can't he just tell Aunt Isobel about us being orphans and wanting to see if we really are Kinlochys. Not that I've ever heard of anyone called Kinlochy before.

Does it really matter if we're Kinlochys and not Mathesons? I like being a Matheson. I've got used to it. Mum and Dad were Mathesons after all. Well I mean we called them Mum and Dad, and that fazes me stupid. I mean to say to find our parents weren't our parents after all.

If I've to be honest – and I'm only talking to myself in this diary so it would be silly really not to be honest – I wish I'd never heard of the name Kinlochy or that we were orphans. 'Cos it means that Aunt Isobel isn't even our aunt. So according to Mac we don't have anyone – no relations. At least back in Jasper we had all our friends.

Oh heck, now I'm going to cry like a real stupid.

★★★★★

Next morning Steve appeared on their doorstep suggesting that the two of them went swimming in the nearby indoor pool. They had barely been walking for five minutes when he raised the subject.

'Mother told me your house was burgled the other night.'

Robert looked at him. 'Yes.'

'Must have upset your aunt.'

'It did – very much,' said Fiona with feeling.

'There've been a number of burglaries round these parts.'

'Oh,' said Robert as they crossed the road towards the Dunkeld Road Swimming Baths.

'Anything special taken?'

Robert looked at Steve and felt that he already knew all about the etui and even the way his room had been ransacked. So what was he trying to discover?

'This and that,' Fiona replied vaguely and gave him such a brilliant smile that he asked no more questions.

The outing had been a success as Fiona told Aunt Isobel over lunch, though, added Robert, it was not the same as swimming in Jasper National Park with the blue sky overhead and the great snowcapped mountains in the backgroud.

'Do you miss Alberta so much?' asked Aunt Isobel kindly.

Tears welled into Fiona's green eyes.

'Cheer up, Fi,' he said.

'It's not that,' she said, sobbing, 'it's all that horrible business over the etui and that sergeant.' She turned and looked at Aunt Isobel. 'Robert didn't do it.'

'Now, now, no one said he did.'

'Of course I didn't,' he declared.

52

Aunt Isobel pushed Fiona's napkin into her hands. 'I do so want you to feel this is your home,' she said, changing the subject.

And for the next two days Aunt Isobel went out of her way to make them feel at home. She told them all about the history of the town, took them down fascinating little backstreet vennels and winding closes in one of which they saw The Old Ship Inn which dated back to 1665. They roamed over old churchyards, Robert peering eagerly at gravestones for the magic name Kinlochy – but always in vain. They had a wonderful picnic one particularly fine day on the Buckie Braes close to Craigie Burn. Another day they saw Pitheavlis Castle near the sparkling Craigie Burn. Built in the mid-1550s by the Ross family of the Craigie Barony it was still being lived in.

Finally, they saw the thirty-foot-high Lynedoch Monument at the Perth Bridge end of the North Inch. This, explained Aunt Isobel, after she had taken a photograph of them beside the monument against a dark blue sky, was erected in 1896 to remember the forming of the Perthshire Volunteers known as 'Graham's Grey Breeks'. Later in 1881 the regiment became the 2nd Battalion of the Cameronians.

It was while Robert was reading the names of the great battles where Graham's Grey Breeks had fought in countries as far afield as America, South Africa and India, that Aunt Isobel announced with a trace of excitement in her voice that she had a surprise for them.

'A surprise,' echoed Fiona, 'we've had nothing but surprises since we came here.'

'Lots of good ones too,' added Robert. 'These trips around Perth – just top grade they've been.'

'Ah, but this is something rather special. And it comes in the shape of a small boy called Benjamin who will be staying with us.'

Fiona's interest was immediately aroused. But Robert felt dumped. He was just getting used to the house and, more particularly, to Aunt Isobel.

Anyone else would be an intruder . . .

He was about to say something when a youngster with a silken-coated spaniel, ears flapping excitedly, raced down to the River Tay.

'Isn't he lovely,' exclaimed Fiona. 'Oh Robert, if only.'

'If only,' echoed Robert, thinking how all his life he had longed for a dog of his own. A companion to take with him on walks, to sit with him at home – wherever home might be.

'The last thing we want is a – ' Aunt Isobel broke off in mid-sentence as she saw the expressions on their faces. Perhaps for all Robert knew she was thinking of when she had been a child and had passionately wanted a pet . . .

He spoke diffidently. 'Remember what Sergeant Ochilston said when he left.'

'Yes,' said Fiona quickly, 'he suggested a dog.'

'So he did,' remarked Aunt Isobel, studying them.

'And I'd look after it – properly. Take it for walks. Oh, Aunt Isobel.' There was all the longing in the world in his voice. 'It would be just great. And you'd have company when we were out.'

'I suppose you were never allowed a dog.'

Robert was puzzled. 'No. How did you guess?'

Aunt Isobel stood by the monument looking back over the wide greenness of the North Inch. 'It was near here that it happened.'

'What happened?' asked Fiona.

'Your mother was carrying a baby at the time – seven months gone she was – and a great black Alsatian rushed up at her. She lost her balance and fell. Something happened – I don't exactly know what – but she lost the baby and could never have another.'

'Poor mummy,' said Fiona. 'If only she had told us.'

'Then I wouldn't have gone on so about it. Every birthday I asked them for a dog.'

'Yes it would have been better but I don't think she could bear to talk about it.'

Suddenly Robert realised what Aunt Isobel had just said. 'She could never have another.' Was that her way of saying gently that she knew they were orphans? Was it just a slip of the tongue? He stood deep in thought pondering the question.

'You're serious all of a sudden,' she said.

'Yes, I was just thinking about what you said then. It all made sense.' Robert paused. Was this the moment to blurt it out? To ask her about their real parents – about the Kinlochys? Excitement welled up in him. He opened his mouth. 'Aunt Isobel – '

Her features warmed with sudden affection. 'Yes, Robert, you can have a dog of your very own.'

Fiona was overjoyed. 'Oh, Aunt Isobel, that's wonderful.'

And realising that he had missed the opportunity to ask her the truth, he in turn expressed his delight. 'Gee, that's just great. That is something.'

'What will we get?' she asked, laughing at his remark.

'A spaniel,' said Fiona, no doubt thinking wistfully of the silken-haired animal which had dashed by and prompted this exciting change in direction of their conversation.

Aunt Isobel was matter of fact. 'Not an Alsatian. Not a big dog.'

'Of course not,' replied Fiona seriously. And she flung herself into Aunt Isobel's arms.

'Bless you, my dear,' said Aunt Isobel.

The rest of the day raced happily by and even when Aunt Isobel sent them off to bed early it did not spoil it. In fact that turned out rather well, for Fiona came and sat on Robert's bed and they talked quietly together about the dog, about Benjamin, about the search for their true identity and about their new life with Aunt Isobel in Perth, but always returning to the search and Robert's plans to visit the Central Registrar's in Edinburgh where the records for the whole of Scotland were filed away.

Then Fiona slipped away to her own room and Robert lay in the darkness looking out at the stars – he could just make out the giant cross of Cygnus flying across the silvery light of the Milky Way.

At first he thought it was his imagination. He lifted his head from the pillow and listened.

Silence. Then the faint murmur of voices rising and falling. Now he sat up and listened more keenly.

Aunt Isobel had a visitor. But he or she had not entered the house by either the front or the back door.

Could it be by a certain window that was left open? A window that faced the secret depths of the back garden. A window that Aunt Isobel would not want locked . . .

Extract from Fiona's diary

Gee, Steve McLarnty is physical. Swimming with his arm round my waist the other day. It was horrible and yet it was – exciting.

But the best part of the day was Mac and me talking together tonight. We're going to have our own dog. Mac thinks that would be 'top grade'. But he's not keen about this boy Benjamin. I guess he feels put out. Mac should have more sense.

I wonder if Benjamin ever plays with Weasel and, if he does, what does he think of him. I watched Weasel when he thought he was not being observed – he just stood there listening to that stereo headset affair and picking his nose. Ooh he was revolting. He gave me the feeling that he was receiving messages and not just listening to a tape or a radio programme. That seems an odd thing to write but that's how I felt.

Steve told me he was a 'genius' with his dad's car – can locate faults in the fuel injection system – I think that's what he said but it means nothing to me – when the garage are really stumped. At least that's human. But gee I wish he'd stop picking his nose like that. It's real snot – that's a joke. I wish I hadn't written that now – it spoils the diary somehow.

Chapter 12
THE ARRIVAL OF BENJAMIN

Benjamin's arrival was watched by a sinister figure

L ong after the murmur of voices was silent, Robert lay awake. It reminded him of
another occasion when he had heard voices in the night, the night his parents were
talking about him. 'We've got to tell the lad the truth. He has a right to it.'

But would he ever find out the truth? Then, unbidden into his mind came that
terrifying picture of mum and dad skiing down to their death . . .

He forced himself to think of these other voices. Aunt Isobel had said she was going
to bed early. Certainly there had been no mention of a visitor. Anyway, why all the
whispering? Had they something to hide?

His thoughts shifted to the visit to the local Registrar's Office and the strange look the
helpful assistant had given him when he had mentioned the name 'Kinlochy'. Afterwards
when he had told Fiona about it she had told him he was 'imagining things'.

Perhaps he was. But he was not imagining voices tonight. He would ask her if she had
heard them. With that thought in mind he fell asleep.

But next morning he did not ask Fiona about the voices. In fact he forgot all about
them – for the time being at any rate. And all because of Benjamin.

Aunt Isobel was quieter than usual as she ladled out porridge onto their plates. 'Now
don't tell me you don't like porridge,' she remarked. 'On a cold day like this it's good
for you.'

And even for a Scottish summer it was a cold day with grey skies and a sharp wind
which had sent his bedroom curtains blowing back into the room, together with a chill
air in the house itself.

Robert tasted the porridge and nearly burned his tongue. It was hot, thick and sticky
with not much taste. Sugar was needed he decided and stretched his hand across the
table to the silver sugar bowl.

Aunt Isobel firmly removed his hand and directed it towards the salt cellar. 'Salt is
what you want, my lad. That's all the seasoning you'll ever need with my porridge.'

He grimaced. 'Salt.'

'Surely not,' exclaimed Fiona as she suspiciously regarded the grey substance on her plate. She poured some milk on. 'Milk helps,' she remarked unthinkingly to Robert, who almost choked with laughter.

As it happened it did help to ease it down his throat. But the addition of salt was not to his taste. Nevertheless he was hungry and he spooned it in. In the meantime, Fiona had managed surreptitiously to sprinkle a little sugar on hers and actually appeared to be enjoying it.

'On a cold winter's day you'll both be thanking me for this,' declared Aunt Isobel. 'It'll set you up for school.'

The thought of school cast a momentary gloom over Robert. School was okay when you knew everyone, when you had your own desk with the caramel toffees in the right-hand corner, the apple next to them, and the latest issue of *The Northwest Skier* to read during the breaks. Now everything and everyone would be new to him.

Robert was well into his second piece of toast and honey – with Aunt Isobel it was always toast and honey, never toast and marmalade or toast and jam – when he became aware that she was talking to them. Immersed in his own thoughts he had not been listening.

'He should be here by 10.30 a.m.,' she was saying.

'Here,' he echoed a little dully.

'Where else?' asked his Aunt with a touch of harshness in her voice. 'He should be here all the summer holidays. I'm sure you'll like him.'

Which meant, thought Robert, that we had better like him.

'What's he like?' asked Fiona with interest, leaning forward elbows on the table and unconsciously licking the honey from her fingers.

Robert wanted to say, 'What's *who* like?' but didn't dare.

Aunt Isobel paused in the middle of pouring herself a second cup of tea – always two cups of tea at breakfast.

'He's a cheeky lad at times. But he's fun and he's bright. I can't abide stupidity. And certainly not in my relations.'

'Oh,' exclaimed Robert innocently, 'so he's a relation.'

'And I certainly cannot abide folk who don't listen – that's the height of bad manners.'

'Sorry, Aunt Isobel, I didn't mean to be rude.'

'No of course you didn't, Robert. He's my brother Jim's only son.'

'Uncle Jim's son. Now I know who you mean.'

Fiona helped him. 'Remember, Benjamin is his name.'

Robert looked blank. He couldn't remember any Benjamin.

Aunt Isobel decided to be patient. 'Very well, we shall start from the beginning. Benjamin is my eleven-year-old nephew, your one and only cousin.'

Robert scowled at her. He didn't like people making a fool of him.

'I'm sorry I couldn't remember his name. But there is no need to treat me like a child.'

Aunt Isobel glared at him. Then she began to smile, her face softened and a twinkle came into her eyes. 'That was quite wrong of me. I'm not at my best this morning, but it is no excuse I know.'

Fiona was instantly sorry. 'Is there anything we can do to help?'

Robert chimed in helpfully. 'Like washing the dishes.'

'Bless you both. You know I think that robbery upset me more than I realised. It was not a pleasant feeling having someone peering round your home like that.'

Robert, remembering the policeman's questions, felt distinctly uncomfortable at his aunt's remarks, but wisely he said nothing.

57

Fiona, for once, was tactful. 'It was really horrible for you, Aunt Isobel, and especially just after we'd arrived.'

Aunt Isobel regarded Robert thoughtfully. 'Yes, as you say especially just after you had arrived. A most unfortunate coincidence.' Then there was another of her sudden changes of mood that still caught Robert unawares. 'But let's forget all about that for now.'

'Yes,' said Robert, glad to shelve the subject.

'Benjamin's mother died of cancer four years ago.'

Robert was contrite. 'Poor fellow,' he said with feeling.

'That must have been really terrible,' added Fiona, her eyes large in her pointed face.

'It was. Terrible too for Jim, who is out of the country for much of the year carrying out his work as a geologist for a large oil company.'

Fiona leaned forward anxiously. 'So what happened to poor old Benjamin?'

'Uncle Jim sent him to a prep school.'

'A boarding school?' asked Robert.

'Yes. There are a number of very fine ones in Scotland, I'm told. Though I'm not for them myself you understand.'

'Why not?' asked Robert.

'We all pay our taxes and our children should all go to state schools the same as everyone else.'

Fiona looked puzzled. 'But what would happen to boys like Benjamin then?'

'The state could run boarding schools just for boys in that position. I don't hold with private education.'

Fiona drank the rest of her tea and again propped her chin in her hands.

'So in the holidays when Uncle Jim is away on some oil rig – '

'Benjamin stays with a school friend or me.'

Again it was Fiona who carried on the conversation. 'And do you like having him Aunt Isobel?'

Robert watched his aunt, awaiting her answer.

'Yes. Very much. As I told you earlier, he's fun.'

But Robert was not so sure that he wanted an eleven-year-old boy in the house – even if he were fun. Of course it was obvious that Aunt Isobel was fond of him. He only needed to look at her when she spoke about Benjamin to see that. Subconsciously a part of him resented the arrival of another boy. He wanted, no needed, to feel that this was his and Fiona's home, that they belonged there, that Aunt Isobel would grow fond of them and that – he glowered into his tea cup, a little surprised at his own train of thought – they would grow fond of her. This thought made him uncomfortable. Boys shouldn't have to feel fond of a grown up, or should they? But after all, mum and dad were dead. Loneliness swept over him.

Then Aunt Isobel did an extraordinary thing. She came round the table and put a hand on each of their shoulders. 'I know what you're thinking. She has known Benjamin for years. She is,' Aunt Isobel paused, 'very fond of him. And so I am. But that does not mean that I cannot be just as fond of new *friends*.'

Friends. Robert's mind echoed the word. Were they not going to be more than friends? Vaguely he realised that *friends*, said with such obvious warmth, meant something special to Aunt Isobel. She was so much more reserved than anyone he had known in Canada that it was difficult to understand her. But Fiona seemed to understand all right. She turned and smiled up at Aunt Isobel.

'That was really nice of you – the way you said *friends*, I mean.'

'Now that is settled let's get down to the business of washing up,' said Aunt Isobel briskly.

Fiona looked hard at Robert. 'Come on, Mac. It's your turn to do the washing up.'

He felt like groaning, partly because he loathed washing up and partly because he was annoyed with himself for being so sentimental. At this rate he would be as bad as Fiona. Nevertheless he got quickly to his feet and went over to the sink. With a masculine show of efficiency he shoved the blue plastic bowl under the tap, turned on the hot water and squirted in the washing-up liquid till the water foamed and bubbled. Out with the brush, in with the dishes, a quick scrub round and onto the draining board.

'We'll finish this in no time,' he declared between clenched teeth. 'I just hope Benjamin can take his turn.'

The bus station was only ten minutes walk away but because he would be bringing his case with him Aunt Isobel took them round in the Citroen.

As they waited, Aunt Isobel's earlier pensive look was replaced with one of eager anticipation. Robert looked up at the grey sky with its deepening clouds and plunged his hands in his jeans' pockets.

'Buck up, Mac.' The words were a half-whisper. 'He'll be really nice. You'll see.'

His normal good nature came to the surface and he smiled.

'I'm sure he will. But it's just that . . . '

He never completed the sentence for at that moment the long bus swung round the corner at the end of Leonard Street and seconds later it had drawn up and the first of the passengers was coming out – an old woman with a stick, helped by an elderly man. Buses always seemed to be full of old people, he thought to himself. More women appeared and then a man who, on leaving the vehicle, immediately pulled out a huge briar pipe and, with his eyes on the doorway, proceeded to light up. He stood there waiting, watching and puffing aggressively while other passengers jostled in growing irritation to get out. A boy appeared at the exit. Abruptly the pipe-smoking man turned and sped swiftly away, but not before the boy had spotted him.

It just had to be Benjamin, lugging a huge case and trying to look casual, thought Robert, recalling how he used to feel when he came home after being away for a short holiday. He stepped forward to help him with the case, studying the figure in crumpled jacket and with tie askew as he did so.

Benjamin had a round face, owlish it was, with round glasses and unruly fair hair. At that moment he was looking suitably serious after a long journey in a bus. The expression, Robert realised with surprise, masked another feeling. Anxiety – fear? He stopped, put down the case with evident relief and looked over at Aunt Isobel. Suddenly the round chubby face broke into a huge grin. He threw out his arms and in a burst of exuberance shouted, 'Yippee a million times. I'm – I'm – I'm on holiday. I'm on holiday.' He raced forward almost throwing himself at Aunt Isobel, all thoughts of making an adult approach evidently forgotten.

Aunt Isobel forgot her usual air of reserve and hugged the small figure unashamedly. 'Oh it is good to see you, Benjamin.'

'And it's g-g-great to see you, Aunt Isobel.' The stutter was not pronounced but was there all the same.

He whirled round and regarded Robert and Fiona with an owlishly solemn expression. Then he pushed his spectacles back with a biro-stained forefinger and gazed even harder at them. Robert could almost see the wheels of his mind going round.

'So these are the newcomers. They're taking over the house. What will they be like? Snooty, friendly?' Robert felt a wave of sympathy for the lad.

'Hi, Benjamin,' he called out cheerfully. 'I'm sure glad to see you.'

'Me too,' added Fiona warmly.

The face remained solemn for a few more seconds as he stepped forward, hand outstretched and Robert realised with amusement that he was actually meant to shake hands. Well, that really was something. He caught the laughter in his sister's eyes but refrained from commenting. The handshaking over, Benjamin suddenly sent a yo-yo whizzing out towards them. Inches from Robert's jacket he drew it back, then flicked it out again, and this time he cheekily stopped it in mid-air just as it was about to strike Fiona on the end of her nose. The yo-yo curled back with magic artistry and disappeared into a pocket, all in a matter of seconds. His face broke into a huge grin. 'Bet you weren't expecting that. I hold the school yo-yo record. S-Seven thousand and f-fifty-nine times I've kept it going. S-Seven thousand and f-fifty-nine.

'Really,' asked Fiona with suitable amazement in her voice.

'Yes. I c-c-could have done it another' – he paused thinking hard – 'ooh another three thousand and sixty-five times. If my arm hadn't s-s-seized up. I couldn't move it for – for days and days. Doc MacIntosh said he'd n-never seen such an arm before.' And he lapsed into silence.

Aunt Isobel added proudly, 'He is the undoubted yo-yo champion of the school. I've never met anyone like him. He plays with it for hours and with such skill.'

Benjamin, enjoying the praise, beamed happily. Robert felt like explaining that he had been the junior school's ski champion three years running. Heck, anyone could play an old yo-yo. The way Aunt Isobel had spoken you'd have thought he was a miracle boy or something.

Fiona might have been reading his thoughts for she scowled at him then turned to smile brilliantly at Benjamin. 'You know, Benjamin, that really is something. Wait till I write to my friends back home that I know a yo-yo champion.'

Robert choked in disgust and debated whether he should pick up the bulging suitcase. Benjamin started to bend down to heave at it but Robert half-relented.

'Mustn't have a yo-yo champ hurting his arm with a case like that,' he said in as deep a voice as he could and yanked at the handle. To his surprise he found he could just lift it and no more. 'It weighs a ton weight,' he said.

'You see it's got my latest collection of Scottish stones in it,' explained Benjamin without apology. 'And there's a g-g-great piece of garnet weighing n-nearly seven pounds.' He paused. 'And a computer from daddy.'

'No wonder it's heavy,' grumbled Robert, adding under his breath, 'I never thought I'd become a porter to a boy who fills his cases with bits of stone.'

Another glance darted from Fiona as he lugged the case off towards the Citroen. Further down the street he caught sight of the pipe-smoking man secretly watching them . . .

'So what are you going to be when you're grown up?'

Uh, thought Robert to himself, that was a condescending enough remark from a fourteen-year-old girl. But Benjamin didn't see it in that light.

He bounced up and down on the balls of his feet. 'I'm going to be g-g-g-ol-ol.' He stopped, his face red. 'A-A-A,' and then speaking very slowly and distinctly, '*an archaeologist*'.

It sounded as if he had been going to say geologist. Well perhaps at that age it did not matter which, thought Robert feeling sorry for a young lad who had to wear glasses and was lumbered with a stammer.

Bronco's doors were open now, Aunt Isobel was behind the wheel and when the car failed to start after the second jab at the starter Robert went and swung the handle. With a jerk and a shake the Citroen rattled into life, dark smoke gushing out of the exhaust.

Benjamin gurgled with delight and banged the bonnet with his fist. 'Good old Bronco,' he shouted.

Fiona was already in the back seat. She knew that Robert liked to sit in the front. Robert saw that Benjamin was standing aside expecting to sit beside their aunt. Robert dived into the back seat. Benjamin grinned at him, then with a serious expression on his round face, sat down and pulled the door closed.

'Off we go, Jim Clark,' he yelled exuberantly, then turning, added for Robert and Fiona's benefit, 'he was a Scot and he won seven Grand Prix races in one year. And that's a record.'

Perhaps Aunt Isobel was determined to live up to the name he had given her because she drove like a demon, eventually speeding through the lights when they were at amber at the junction with York Place. The morning traffic was quite heavy in Caledonian Road but that seemed to make no difference and with frenzied concentration she jumped the little car from one lane to another.

Then it was all over: the car turned down several streets and shortly afterwards coasted to a halt outside their home. Aunt Isobel switched off the engine with a characteristic flourish and the last tremors of the Citroen died away into silence.

Benjamin bounded out like a jack-in-a-box.

'Yippee, I'm home,' he cried. And he danced a little jig of sheer delight.

Robert had not wanted to share their new home with anyone. So he sat in the back seat and scowled. And when the sun came bursting out from behind a cloud and Aunt Isobel exclaimed brightly, 'Definitely a fine day, ' his scowl deepened. Fiona, who knew his moods, looked anxious. 'Come on, Mac,' she implored. 'We're all home.'

He turned his head away and looked out of the window. Then he got out of the car, felt the warmth of the sun and saw the look of happiness on Benjamin's face.

'Come on, old sober sides,' said Fiona.

'S-S-Sober s-s-sides,' echoed Benjamin grinning and flicking out his yo-yo with a flourish.

'Mac,' Fiona's voice was pleading.

He looked at the small figure in front of him. Specs, stammer, 'A swot probably,' he muttered.

★★★★★

Benjamin gobbled his food down, stuttering in his excitement, telling them all about his computer and a new boy at school, an Indian called Suman. 'His f-f-family go back hundreds of years,' he told them.

Robert wondered how many hundreds of years the Kinlochys went back. Further than the Mathesons?

Now Benjamin was asking Aunt Isobel all about her photography. How many had she taken? How many had she had published? Questions and numbers. That was the way it was with Benjamin.

Indeed, after lunch he had Robert quite bewildered with his explanations of his computer and its memory. Fiona of course did not even pretend to follow half of it. 'I'm not much good at that kind of thing,' she explained.

Benjamin looked as if he felt sorry for her. 'Can't you do anything then?'

Robert did not know whether to laugh or be annoyed. 'She can paint,' he said at last. 'Top grade stuff too. Perhaps she'll paint you one day.'

Benjamin grinned but somehow the grin never reached his eyes.

'Wouldn't you like that?' asked Robert feeling puzzled.

'S-Someone drew me at school.'

'And?' asked Fiona.

Benjamin's features creased. 'It was just a g-gigantic pair of s-spectacles.'

In that instant Robert felt intensely angry: angry with himself for his earlier reactions to the young lad and now angry with some stupid idiot for being so insensitive. But he could not find the right words.

So it was left to Fiona. 'But gee, Benjamin, your specs make you look really wise and clever.'

'You think so?'

'Sure I do. Anyway don't you remember the story of the ugly duckling?'

Robert groaned inwardly. Now she was being tactless, but Benjamin did not see it that way. 'Yes, of course.'

'Well then Benjy – I may call you Benjy sometimes?'

Again the face lit up. 'Please Fiona.'

'When you're older, Benjy, and your features have all sharpened up you will look great. And it will be partly thanks to those glasses of yours. Except of course they'll be bolder, darker frames and sort of oblong. Not round.'

'You m-mean that?'

'Sure I do. And just to prove it I'll draw you as you'll look in – ' she paused.

'Six years time.'

So Fiona got her sketch-pad and, head on one side, chewing a piece of fair hair, she rapidly drew an older Benjamin. And sure enough he did look great. Benjamin was touchingly grateful.

'I'll keep this always and always. And when people call me s-speccy I'll remember that this is what I'll l-look like one day.'

He studied the drawing, eyes owlishly thoughtful behind the glasses, and Robert thought to himself. 'He's top grade.'

'Now it's laughing time,' and the imp was in his eyes again.

'I wonder what it would be like to laugh a million and one times.'

'Why a million and one times?' asked Robert.

'Ah well that's quite different from a million.'

Fiona stood up. 'It is?'

'Of course. Everyone talks of m-millions. Millions of this and that but never a million and one. So it's different and anyway I like the sound of a million and one laughs.' He paused and gazed seriously at Fiona. 'Now I'm going to start laughing and you can count.'

'How do you count a laugh?'

Benjamin wrinkled his nose.

'After all,' said Robert, 'laughs can go on for a long time – I reckon when you laugh they do.'

'Yes, and you can have short sort of bursts of laughter,' added Fiona.

'All right,' said Benjamin. 'A two-second laugh.'

'How am I going to count it?' asked Robert playing along with the younger lad.

'That's easy. Count one yo-yo, two yo-yo.'

So Benjamin laughed and Fiona counted. Then they all laughed together. Curiously enough it was Benjamin who stopped first. 'We're all friends now.'

'Gee, of course we are, Benjamin.'

'But why do you say that?' asked Fiona looking perplexed.

Benjamin rubbed the side of the yo-yo against his cheek.

'W-Well when I met you, Robert looked . . . ' His voice trailed off.

Robert felt guilty.

62

'When you got out of the car you looked browned off,' said Benjamin firmly.
'Forget it, Benjamin.' Then for no reason at all Robert added. 'But what about you when you were getting off that bus – you looked sort of worried.'
A shadow crossed the young lad's face. 'I thought I'd seen someone,' he muttered. Instinct told Robert who it was. 'The guy with the pipe.'
'Yes, you saw him too.'
'A slimy creepy guy,' said Fiona.
'He was w-watching me on the journey.'
'Just a nasty creep,' said Robert. Then wanting to change the subject added, 'But now you're here we're sure going to have a top grade time.'
Out came the yo-yo. Out came that infectious laugh. But a shadow of memory clouded Benjamin's eyes and Robert wondered again just what the pipe-smoking man's interest was in Benjamin and, for that matter, in Fiona and himself. Was his arrival on the same bus just a coincidence or was there something more sinister behind it?

Extract from Fiona's diary

Cousin Benjamin has installed himself here at Arisaig. He's nuts about yo-yos, has a stutter and wears gig lamp glasses. At least that's how you would describe him when you've just met him. But it would only be half a picture – like leaving out all the colour.

He also laughs a lot but I think he needs lots of affection. He showed me his computer but it meant nothing to me. Oh yes, and he had a dinky little recorder that you can slip into your pocket. He said it belonged to his father but he got a new one so he gave this one to Benjamin.

It seems to me his dad – yes it should be dad and not father – gives him lots of presents but is never around when needed. Perhaps that's what happens to archaeologists . . .

He and Aunt Isobel are real close. She's like a mother to him. I noticed that when they were talking together he almost lost his stutter altogether.

Tonight Aunt Isobel told me I'd got real talent. She has kept asking to see my 'portfolio' so I decided I must not play too shy or she would forget to ask me again. Anyway it was specially sweet of her to ask when Benjamin had just arrived.

So I showed it to her and she was really nice about my paintings. Intelligent too. All this photography has given her an eye for composition so she is really quite good.

Later she promised to show me some of her landscape photos. But she didn't go and do that right away like most people just to show how clever she is. No, she said she would wait till another day.

I thought that was really nice of her.

Now I want to work out a chess problem.

P.S. I had to take one of Aunt Isobel's 'wee peeks' at the solution because I'm not good at back-rank mates.

Chapter 13
OSSIAN'S HALL

*Cheryl warned, 'Velly noisy here. You
could fire gun and no one hear.'*

Looking back on that fateful day when death stalked his footsteps as he followed
the winding woodland path high above the foaming River Braan, Robert was never
quite sure why he had gone in the first place.

Steve had appeared on the doorstep leaning casually against the side of the doorway.

'What about us cycling up to the Hermitage? Mother's put a picnic together for me.'

Robert had been suspicious, though the idea had appealed. After all, only a short time
earlier he had been studying an old atmospheric print of the Hermitage and reading
about it in Sarah Murray's book *The Beauties of Scotland*, written in 1799. She had
described the River Braan forcing its way through a rocky channel, referred to its 'foaming
rage at the falls just above' and gone on to write 'the noise of the cascade is excessive'.

He wondered what the Hermitage would look like today.

'I've got no bike.'

'No problem, Rob, I've got the use of a friend's.'

Robert felt he was being pressurised. 'I'm not Rob.'

'No sweat. Robert. Ask your aunt to make you a picnic.'

Robert still felt undecided.

'Fi told me you were mad about history and all that stuff. We could look at Ossian's
Cave.'

That finally persuaded him but he still could not fathom Steve's motive. Historic
buildings, caves, walks in the woods, even just enjoying nature, these were not Steve
McLarnty's scene. So why bother to invite him out for the day? Just to be nice to him?
And when on earth had Fiona – damn him calling her Fi – ever told him about his
interest in old Scotland?

Aunt Isobel had echoed Robert's own misgivings. 'It seems out of character to me,'
she had said. 'But it is a fine spot. You should enjoy it.'

'I wondered about a picnic.'

'Of course. Give me quarter of an hour, Robert, and you'll be out from under my
feet.'

'Gee thanks, Aunt Isobel. But what about Benjamin?'

'Don't worry your head about him. He's going to show Fiona the harbour this morning. In the afternoon he can give Bronco a polish and help me with some printing.'

Robert shrugged on the nylon haversack containing the picnic and two cans of Coke together with sheath knife, a length of nylon rope, sun shades and his old compass. He grinned to himself as he thought nostalgically of those long summer days off up to Cottonwood Creek or way down to Miette Hotsprings on Highway 16. In his mind he could smell the fragrant resin of the great forests of Englemann spruce and Lodgepole pine.

He realised that the River Braan so vividly described by Sarah Murray would only be a tiddler compared with the mighty Athabasca River as it hurled its foaming way through a gorge of solid quartzite, and yet this was the country of his birth and it was here that he had chosen to make his home, so tiny hillside streams, woods covering only a few acres, five, perhaps ten-mile-long nature trails and towns like Perth steeped deep in history were now part of his heritage. And it was time to get to know them so that they became as much a part of his being as the mountains, valleys and lakes of Alberta.

With these thoughts in mind he helped adjust the saddle of the bicycle Steve had produced for him. It was still cool with a light breeze but the sun was behind them warming their backs as they pedalled up the A9 towards Dunkeld. As they strained on the pedals on the long gradient alongside Bankfoot, and Steve puffed and sweated, Robert grinned. It was obvious that Steve was not used to this kind of thing and was finding it punishing work.

'Let's walk a bit,' he suggested.

Robert eyed the horizon. 'We've only a hundred yards to the top. I vote we keep going.'

Steve gritted his teeth and looked like snarling a rude reply but he refrained and struggled on, sweat pouring down his face. Robert was now beginning to feel the strain and wondered if it had been wise to push Steve to this extent. Would he not find a way to get his own back . . .

The sun was higher and hotter as they passed the road on their right towards the ancient town of Dunkeld. A little further on and they turned off to the left and bumped over a short stretch of rough country road to the Hermitage car park.

Steve wiped the sweat off his face with the sleeve of his shirt and stood bow-legged for a minute.

'I'd forgotten how far it was.'

But Robert reckoned he had never cycled here before, been taken in a car – yes! They padlocked their cycles to the wooden railing and walked over towards the bridge under the single railway line. On the left was a stone shelf containing green leaflets on the Hermitage Woodland Walk produced by the National Trust for Scotland. Above was a slot for coins and an invitation to pay 25 pence.

Steve, after glancing over his shoulder to see that there was no one else in the car park, took a couple of leaflets.

'Might as well have one.'

'What about paying?'

'You must be dumb, man. Pay for one of these? They should be giving them away.'

'But that's cheating,' protested Robert, pulling out some coins from his trouser pocket and carefully putting in two tens and a fivepence – still strange money to him.

'Go take a running jump at yourself,' said Steve crudely and strolled off under the bridge.

Robert stood wondering if he should pay for Steve's copy as well. Finally he shrugged his shoulders and, notching his thumbs under his haversack straps, set off with the long easy stride characteristic of a true hillwalker. He easily caught up with Steve, enjoying the soft springy feel of the ground under his running shoes.

At this point the River Braan with its alder-lined bank flowed smoothly but soon ahead of them Robert could hear it rushing through narrow-necked gorges. His keen countryman's eyes spotted yew, elm and beech trees and, of course, everywhere the tall, marvellously straight Douglas conifers, one of which he noted from a small notice was 164 feet high.

'Quite a height,' remarked Steve, trying to be conversational.

But Robert, recalling the towering height of the conifers in Jasper National Park, was not in a conciliatory mood. 'That's nothing. In 1895 a man in Vancouver felled a Douglas fir 417 feet high.'

'You know something,' grated Steve, 'you make me sick with all that talk of what a great country Canada is.'

Robert found himself defending it in spite of himself. 'And so it is – a great country.'

'So why did you leave it then?'

'To come and live with Aunt Isobel. She's our only relative apart from Benjamin's father and he's abroad most of the time.'

'Oh tell that to your grandmother.' Steve stooped, picked up a fir-cone and threw it into the river below. 'You had a reason for coming here. That's what Pete says and I think he's right.'

Robert looked hard at the bigger boy, measuring his superior height and weight. 'Just what do you mean by that, Steve McLarnty?'

Steve opened his mouth to say something. Then a wary look came into his eyes. 'You know full well what I'm getting at.'

Robert felt himself growing white with anger and fear that the Weasel and Steve somehow did know. But how could they?

'Do I?'

'Aw come off it. Don't look so innocent.'

Robert shrugged, refusing to give anything away. 'Come back a bit and watch the dipper swimming under water.'

'What's a dipper for Hell's sake?'

'You don't know and you've been here before?'

Steve looked suddenly abashed. 'Not for some time I haven't.'

Robert let his explanation pass. 'A dipper is a sort of mixture of wren and blackbird. It can swim and dive and walk along the bottom of the river there and grub about for insects.'

'You're having me on.'

'No, honest I'm not. Come on and I'll show you.'

They stood in silence studying the river but there was no sign of the dipper anywhere. Then Robert spotted a salmon gathering its strength before making a leap up the waterfall.

He was about to point it out when the dipper flew straight under the bridge to land only yards away on a stone near the other side of the bank.

'There it is. Now watch.'

Sure enough it dived into the water, ducked its head then the whole of its body under the water and emerged seconds later.

'Now I'll show you something,' remarked Steve and began walking back along the path towards the railway bridge. 'Ever seen a tree with seven trunks before?'

Robert admitted he hadn't.

'Have you got a knife on you and I'll carve my initials.' Steve's eyes grew hot. 'And Fi's.'

'You damned well won't,' declared Robert sharply.

Steve's look smouldered but only for a while. 'Forget it. I was only joking. I'll just cut my own initials.'

'Not with my knife, you won't.'

'Well why not for crazy's sake?'

'Because it will damage the tree. That's something the rangers in Jasper National Park were always telling us. The white bit under the bark carried the tree's nourishment and if you cut it deeply this stops it and the tree suffers.'

'And you worry about a tree.'

'Sure, it gives them pain.'

'You're nuts. You really are. A tree's just a piece of wood.' He laughed. 'That's all it is, a piece of wood.'

'But so long as it's growing, it's alive and if I cut your arm it would hurt you.'

'Have it your own way, Robert,' Steve said lazily. 'Come on up to the Hermitage.'

By now several people were beginning to wander through the wood, one or two Americans among them. As they approached the bridge, built in the 1700s, Robert was surprised to see a familiar figure in faded cords, patched tweed jacket and tinted glasses standing with a Chinese girl and gazing into the turmoil of water pouring down the narrow gorge. He followed Steve onto the bridge but when the couple showed no sign of moving Steve muttered something under his breath and abruptly turned and, pushing past Robert, climbed up the path towards the Hermitage or Ossian's Hall, as it is more commonly known.

Robert had the distinct feeling that Steve had wanted them away from the bridge but he could not think why. They entered the folly built in 1758 and stood at the railing with the spray keening through the air and the great roar of the tumbling water filling their ears.

Steve leaned over the railing and pointed towards the water.

'Hey, there's your dipper again.'

Robert was surprised that it should be flying so near the waterfall and began to lean forward. Steve's arm touched his on the railing. At that moment an oriental girl's voice interrupted them.

'Excuse me please, could you take photograph?'

Steve cursed under his breath and Robert, drawing back from the railing above the almost perpendicular face of the rocks above the foaming water, turned. Tweed Jacket was holding out his camera, his free hand on his throat.

'I've lost my voice,' he croaked.

The girl gestured to them. 'Please, my fiancé and I – we will stand there, but back a bit. I think it not safe the way you were leaning over.'

Tweed Jacket's face was without expression but his eyes flashed intelligence – and a message, a warning. Steve had been uncomfortably close. He was larger, stronger. But Robert knew that was nonsense . . .

He looked steadily back at Tweed Jacket. 'Thank you,' he said, just loud enough to be heard above the roar of the water.

He took the camera and when the couple were standing with their backs to the railing, carefully pointed it and pressed the shutter release.

'Thank you – so kind of you.' She bowed a comic half-bow that had Steve smirking openly.

The girl pointed to the text of the little green National Trust leaflet. 'Much safer in old days when mirrors reflected everything. Very much safer. Then you see all around you.'

Robert nodded. It was difficult to make out the heavily accented voice against the accoustically amplified sound of the water.

'Velly noisy, you hear nothing at all.' She smiled at them. 'You could fire gun and no one hear. Bang bang!'

'Come on let's get out of here and leave that stupid twit.'

'Goodbye,' Robert said, following Steve out into the trees. Sunlight dappled them as they walked and, over to his right, away from the River Braan, a chaffinch piped its joyous rhythmical song 'chip chip chip, cherry-erry-erry'. The roar of the river seemed muted. There was a momentary stillness and Robert felt he must have imagined everything – the expression in those oriental eyes, the warning in the voice, the sudden closeness of Steve.

'Hear that chaffinch, Steve, there's a happy bird for you.'

Steve grunted a monosyllabic reply and kept walking. Robert shrugged and followed a few paces behind. Soon they had reached a cave, so natural looking that for a moment Robert was completely taken in.

'Ossian's Cave,' announced Steve and stood back to watch Robert's reaction.

Great rocks and slabs of stone indeed made a cave, complete with entrance, peepholes and a wide stone seat.

'Benjamin would think this terrific. It's almost perfect.'

Robert looked up in time to catch the superior expression on Steve's face. 'Fooled you this time and no mistaking.'

Robert smacked a clenched fist into his right hand with annoyance. 'And to think that I thought it was real.'

'Manmade,' said Steve smugly.

And now that Robert studied it he realised that it was just perfect, too perfect not to have been constructed by man. He felt disappointed, cheated.

Behind him a voice which he instantly recognised said, 'Velly clever indeed.' The high-pitched oriental voice added. 'These boys – they are taken for ride.'

Steve positively scowled at them. 'I wasn't. Not me.' He pointed at Robert. 'But he was taken in all right. Bet you don't have one of these in Canada.'

Robert kept quiet because he couldn't think of a suitable reply and that in itself galled him more than ever. He didn't like to be made a fool of, especially by Steve. Of course if Fiona had been there she would have made him laugh at himself, but she wasn't and he was annoyed. For some unknown reason he felt he had lost face with Tweed Jacket and that in itself was an odd way of thinking. So he decided he was being stupid again. Without looking at either of them he followed Steve along the winding path through a stretch of Norway spruce, and a few yards further on caught sight of a red squirrel sitting high on a branch, its forepaws twirling a pine cone while it stripped it.

The squirrel suddenly froze, its eyes watching them. Robert stood perfectly still but as soon as Steve spotted the little animal he bent down, picked a stone and threw it with surprising accuracy. But the squirrel was just that bit quicker: it dropped the cone and in a flash had vanished up the tree.

'Nearly got you,' said Steve glaring up at the tree.

Robert felt anger boiling up inside him. 'That was a red squirrel you idiot. They're rare. They should be protected from people like you.'

Steve leered at him. 'You are a good little boy aren't you. Proper Aunty's darling.'

Robert wheeled on Steve. 'Go to hell.'

Steve mimicked him. 'Go to hell. So now we're swearing. Oh, we are brave aren't we?'

Robert would have gone for him there and then but at that instant a couple, who had been approaching unseen by the two boys, asked to be allowed to go by on the path. Angrily, Robert stood to one side and Steve smirking to himself turned off the path and made towards the river again.

'This place is crawling with people,' he said.

'They've just as much right to be here as we have.'

'There we go again,' he chanted. 'What a good little boy we have here.' He looked mockingly round at him and Robert began to wonder if Steve were deliberately taunting him.

He shrugged his shoulders. 'Let's eat someplace. I'm starving.'

'Suits me.' He began to walk more purposefully. 'I know just the place for us. Above the river, out of the way of all these people cruising around here.'

At the back of his mind a warning bell rang – but so faintly that Robert hardly noticed it.

'Sounds great. We might even see the dipper again. Across the railroad from us on the Athabasca River Fiona and I were lucky enough to see a kingfisher fly for hundreds of yards upstream.' They had been good days, those long summer days in July and August. He sighed for the past, squared his shoulders and wondered just what the future would bring.

'Over here,' shouted Steve against the growing roar of the river racing through a steep narrow gorge below. Steve plunged through some low-lying shrubs and Robert nearly tripped over a stump of a tree trunk close to the edge of what, in effect, was a small cliff-face. The rock was sharp and sheer and not a great distance from the boiling water below, but Robert could see that it was treacherous: underneath the foam would be jagged rocks. Immediately below him a stunted willow seemed to grow out of a tiny recess. The sun glinted on its leaves and he felt its heat on his forehead and the backs of his hands.

Carefully he stood back a little as he slipped the haversack from his shoulders while Steve did likewise.

'Not a bad spot,' he shouted, trying to make conversation.

Steve's voice slurred over the words. 'It'll serve its purpose.'

Behind him he thought he heard the sound of snapping wood but it was difficult to tell. A cloud came over the sun and he shivered. Abruptly an air of menace hung over him. He felt endangered but from exactly what he could not tell. Steve was unconcernedly munching a roll filled with tomato and egg which was being squeezed out at the sides onto his hands, and was then dripping onto his trousers. No wonder Aunt Isobel thought he was a lout!

Neither spoke for a while and when Robert was rummaging around for the chunk of Madeira cake which had got separated from the rest of the picnic, his hand came in contact with the fine coil of nylon rope. He looked at it and then across at Steve but the latter was now biting deep into a huge wadge of cream cake, his attention well away from Robert.

Later, whenever he looked back at this moment, he wondered what made him do it. Nothing rational: that was for certain. True there was that faint prickling of fear at the back of his neck, but that did not explain why he secretively removed the rope and stuffed it in his trouser hip pocket. The knife, for no other rational reason, he left in the haversack.

He zipped open a can of Coke and, tilting his neck back, drained it in one long glorious swallow. Then the sun came out, beating down upon them and he began to feel drowsy. Leaning his head back on the haversack he let his eyes close. He was back on the Athabasca River watching the kingfisher. Dad was fishing downstream; mum reading a novel; Fiona reflectively chewing a piece of grass and sketching the distant snow-capped mountains.

Robert felt so happy at the thought of being re-united with the family that he could have cried. But there was the strange lopsided reality of a dream, that would slowly dissolve into a nightmare. And so it did. First the sunshine faded, then its friendly warmth, then the familiar scene. The dying away of the sun heralded a cold breeze which whipped across the water.

He opened his eyes and felt rather than saw the atmosphere of menace pressing all around him. Steve had been looking behind him. Now he glanced across.

'Wakey, wakey, ' he called. 'Up on your feet and look at the river now.'

Still bemused with sleep he got up, stepped forward, caught his left foot on the tree stump, staggered, and then felt a slight push as if a blast of wind had struck him. Steve seemed to be putting out a hand to stop him falling but he pitchdived forward.

Below him the turbulent water was surging through the narrow gulley of rocks. A faint cry rang out above him. Spray struck him. The sheer rock face rushed past and a terrifying kaleidoscope of impressions – sounds and pictures – whirled round him.

Instinctively his arms had gone out, and a subconscious memory of the small willow prompted him to take action. His hands grasped at the branches, his arms were being wrenched out of their sockets, and finally there was a blinding crack on the head.

Extract from Fiona's diary

I've only been writing my diary for a few days and already I sort of associate it with something I do before going to bed. But now I wonder. Is there any reason why I have to wait till then? I mean can't I just write down something when I feel like it?

After all I might forget something at night and more important I might not catch the sort of mood of the moment. Hey, that's a good phrase for me. Mood of the moment.

Now I've written this – it's one thirty and I've just cleared away the dishes – I feel it's perhaps sort of silly. Perhaps I should just persevere and write whenever the feeling comes over me.

Benjamin has been playing with his computer. Well working away at it – or whatever. He's quite keen.

It's odd but I get the idea that he's worried about that pipe-smoking fellow who was on the bus with him the other day. He started talking about it this morning and then all of a sudden when I asked him a question he closed up like a clam and wouldn't say another word.

I was thinking about that rhyme a few minutes ago. I can't make head or tail of it. It's a silly old rhyme really but mum or dad – I never knew which – must have had a reason for keeping it.

> *When weight of paper is like stone*
> *And flashing claymore is all alone*
> *A myriad pattern of pinpoints green*
> *Create a Scottish map that must be seen.*

Chapter 14
TREACHEROUS
WATERS

The next moment Robert was falling onto
jagged rocks in the River Braan

Pain. Shooting stars bursting inside his skull. A deafening roar of nearby water. Total bewilderment.

Then memory creeping back into his conscious mind. The feeling of being pushed by wind – or human hand. He could not tell, especially as Steve had been several feet away. But where was Steve now? Had he gone for help?

Robert's arms were wrapped round the tree, his legs dangling in space. He looked down at the racing torrent only feet away. He began to be afraid. Looking up he could see no way out. And below . . . ugh! He shouted but there was no hope of anyone hearing him. In time he was bound to fall, and even if a search party came soon there was no guarantee that they would spot him, for the rock above overhung his body by several inches.

Cautiously, he edged his way out along the branch. It began to bend and creak with his weight. With equal caution he edged back towards the safety of the rock face.

Robert huddled there, frightened and in pain. He was trapped.

But then he remembered: there was a length of fine nylon rope tucked into his hip pocket – unless it had fallen out. He removed his right hand from the branch and immediately felt off balance. Hastily he grabbed it again, sweat breaking out on his forehead.

Carefully he tightened his grasp with his left hand and, trying to keep his weight forward, he pushed his right hand into his hip pocket.

His fingers touched the nylon coil and he gasped with relief. Gradually he inched it out, occasionally having to grab hold of the branch again to regain his balance.

Finally the green-coloured rope was in his hand. Now he had to uncoil it. But he could not free both hands and he was terrified that he would drop it.

He pushed the end into his mouth, bit tightly and, with his right hand, undid it.

Painstakingly he tied a slip-knot round the branch as close to its roots as possible. Then he paused and the next part of his plan began to formulate. There was an element

71

of risk but with luck and care he would escape with his life. He would be soaked of course. He might even break an ankle or a rib but he would survive.

The next step was to tie the rope round his waist and ensure that the knot was secure. He tested it and the knot round the branch. Finally satisfied, he let the rope fall into the water and watched with fascinated horror as it was whisked away round a corner in a whirlpool of foam and out of sight. Just so long as there was enough rope . . . That was something he had to gamble on.

He removed his left hand from the branch and took hold of the rope. Then he did the same with his right hand. His body swung free and even as the rope began to slip through his fingers he curled his legs round it and trapped part of it between his feet.

With his right foot clamped firmly on top left and the rope caught in between and with his head throbbing from the blow against the cliff-face, he lowered himself till he was almost doubled up in a crouching position. Then with his feet slightly apart to let the rope ease through, then feet together and one hand over another, he went down and down until the swirling water was up to his knees.

It was too late to realise he should have tried to remove his sneakers and tie them round his neck.

Now the water was up to his waist and the current was dragging him downstream. His grip on the rope tightened. This was literally his lifeline. Let go and he would be in dire trouble.

Robert's feet touched the bed of the river. He braced himself against the surging force of the water. He tried a few steps, with the rope held taut in his hands. Then the water dashed him against a rock, his legs buckled and in an instant he was falling. The water closed in over his head. He gulped in a great mouthful, felt himself choking, panicking, but somehow he held on to the rope.

He struggled to the surface, regained his balance, edged his way to the bank and half-crouched there. It was proving harder than he had expected and there was no sign of a break in the steep, sheer face of rock above him.

Robert knew he could not remain there much longer. He was soaked to the skin and shivering with fear and cold. He ventured back into the water and took a few steps, but was dashed away again by the torrent, water washing over him. But still he had the rope round his waist and in his hand.

Fighting every inch of the way against the current he struggled through a narrow, if not too steep, gorge. Then ahead he saw a waterfall only a few feet high but absolutely vertical.

Beyond that was a pool and lower down he could see rocks at one side of the river – a possible haven till he could attract someone's attention.

But first he had to negotiate the waterfall. As he braced himself he could not know just how difficult it was going to prove.

A few steps later he discovered that he had nearly come to the end of the rope. He stood there, heart thumping against his chest, head throbbing. Carefully he measured the remaining length of rope with his eye and compared it with the distance to the top of the waterfall.

Robert looked back up the river but there was no escape there.

He battled to the top of the waterfall. There were two, maybe two and half feet of rope left. Suddenly he lost his balance. The water surged against him. His feet were off the ground. Another second and he was going to be swept over to almost certain death, for with the rope still tied firmly round his waist he would hang under the full onslaught of the water. A minute, two at the most, and he would be drowned.

He hauled desperately on the rope, dragged himself back, agonising inch upon agonising inch, away from the edge. But his strength was ebbing fast. He gulped down water and felt it blinding his eyes.

Another heave and he was standing leaning into the current, safe for a brief moment at least.

Then he took the decision which would mean life or death.

He smiled grimly to himself. If he survived, and now it was a very questionable 'if', it would sound melodramatic to put it that way but Robert was in no doubt of the seriousness of what he was about to do.

Deliberately he removed his right hand from the rope, felt the almost intolerable strain on his left hand and arm, and fumbled frantically with the knot round his waist.

If it had been an ordinary hemp rope it would have become so sodden that he would not have stood a chance of releasing it, but nylon rope was quite different. Slippery yes, but capable of being eased out of the knot.

First though he had to get some slack on the rope between his hand and his waist. Gritting his teeth, head down against the spray, he shoved himself against the water. But he did not move an inch. The rope remained taut. He tried again. And again. Then he managed to gain a few inches, which was enough for his purpose. He loosened the knot, slipped it free and wrapped the end round his left wrist.

Cautiously he paid it out. A second later and he was being swept over the edge and the water was flowing over him in a solid torrent. Desperately he hung on, dangling only feet above the pool below.

It was now or never. His arms were fully outstretched and the last inches of rope were slipping through his fingers.

Robert let go.

He was thrown backwards into the water and it was that which saved his life for immediately below him a jagged rock lay concealed below the surface.

His feet struck the bed of the pool but the impact was such that his legs buckled. His shoulders and head went under but with a tremendous effort he fought his way to the surface.

He gasped in air, trod water, then, feeling as though he had been through a mangle, struck out with what little strength he had left for the bank: his arms weakly flayed the surface of the pool while his legs dragged behind him. His head went under.

The bank was only a few strokes away. Valiantly he strove to keep himself from sinking. Suddenly he found he had no strength left. He was going down, the water streaming into his lungs.

So this was what it was like to drown. An effortless giving-up of all struggle. No more fighting the rushing torrents. Drifting downwards. Relaxed, at peace . . .

In the recesses of his mind a thought stirred as he was about to lose consciousness. He was a Kinlochy and he had a quest: he had to find out who his parents were.

Letting himself drown was a nonsense. For the lack of one last effort he would die and the quest with him.

Grimly he fought his way to the surface and splashed to the bank. He lay there gasping in air in the afternoon sunshine. There was a voice in his head shouting for help. Help! He wondered dully who it was. His mouth was opening and closing. It was he who was shouting.

Then he was no longer shouting. There was silence.

Chapter 15
A WORD OF WARNING

Dark glasses hid the expression in Tweed Jacket's eyes, but there was no mistaking the warning note in his voice

The shivering would not stop. His muscles contracted, twitched, spasmed. His whole body shook. His teeth clattered like castanets.

But thank God, he was alive . . .

He was dimly conscious of movement, then engine noise, gear-changing, the blast of a horn, the singsong voice of the Chinese girl . . .

Then texture – rough tweed against his face and being carried upstairs. Aunt Isobel's voice was faint and distant and Tweed Jacket speaking in a husky voice that faded in and out of his conscious mind like a poor signal on the short-wave band.

'Please let me know how he is, Miss Matheson. Courageous lad. Showed great initiative.'

The girl's voice, 'Velly strange thing to happen . . .'

Soup, scalding hot was being poured down his throat and he was drifting into a deep slumber . . .

But always shivering – shiver, shiver . . .

Consciousness. A doctor was examining him. 'Nasty knock on the head but it will mend. The shock will not have done the lad any good either.'

Aunt Isobel speaking. 'But he will be all right?'

'Good heavens yes. A good night's sleep – nature's cure you know and he will be up and about.'

The voices faded.

A door opening. 'Mac. Are you all right?'

He mumbled indistinctly.

'Robert, can I come in?'

He smiled at the image of that solemn, laughing india-rubber ball of a boy called Benjamin. 'Yes.'

They were standing looking at him – Fiona biting her underlip and Benjamin looking owlish behind his glasses. Both were worried.

He looked at them through half-closed eyes and knew that he must make them smile.

'One thousand and one laughs.'

'In one minute flat,' replied Benjamin, his face all smiles. He opened his mouth and began laughing. Then Fiona laughed. Finally Robert laughed.

★★★★★

Slowly he opened his eyes. It was ten o'clock in the morning. The pain at the back of his head was now only a subdued throbbing. More importantly, that awful non-stop shivering had finally halted.

Robert sat up. Not so good. He felt a little dizzy at first and there was a drummer beating away inside his head. He lay back and memories of the fateful walk in the Hermitage wood began to filter into his mind. There were gaps at first. He could not, for instance, remember exactly what had happened just before he had fallen over the edge of the bank. Why had he fallen?

Then there had been the nightmarish feeling as the water closed over his head when the full force of the raging torrent had struck him. Gradually he began to piece together the events of the day from the moment Steve had appeared on his doorstep, including the quarrels about the squirrel and Steve wanting to carve his initials and Fiona's on the tree trunk.

Then he recalled Ossian's Hall itself and being taken in by the manmade cave. Little incidents like fine parts of a mosaic flitted across his mental vision.

Tweed Jacket and the Chinese girl were on the bridge and he recalled his surprise at seeing him there. The warning – or was that just imagination – in Ossian's Hall. The look in his eyes. 'Bang, bang,' that was the girl's singsong Chinese accent.

Then he was falling again over the edge. That memory was to return to haunt him for a long time to come. He closed his eyes to shut it out but it became even more vivid. So he concentrated on the hands of the clock beside him and gradually that particular nightmare was pushed back into the recesses of his mind.

There was a knock and Fiona came in carrying a tray with his breakfast. Behind her was the owlish face of Benjamin.

'And how is the invalid today?' asked Fiona, playing the nurse.

'Surviving.' Robert struggled into a sitting position and tenderly felt the back of his head. 'Guess I'll live another day.'

The impish expression that he was getting to know so well crossed Benjamin's face. He whipped out his yo-yo and zoomed it out over Robert's bed with such speed that instinctively the invalid ducked and the pain in his head seemed to explode.

'No more of that,' he groaned.

Benjamin, instantly contrite, pocketed the offending object, bowed twice and shook hands with himself. It was all so solemn that Robert smiled in spite of the pain.

'Five hundred and forty smiles.'

'Five,' retorted Robert who, in rapid succession, contorted his face for the benefit of the younger lad.

Bejamin looked disappointed. Then he pointed at the breakfast tray.

'You've got two boiled eggs today.'

'Aunt Isobel,' began Fiona, still with her nursing voice, 'believes that plenty of food will cure anything.'

Robert grinned. 'I won't argue with that.'

'I only had one egg,' began Benjamin.

At that moment Aunt Isobel entered. 'What's all this about having one egg?'

Benjamin bowed and retreated to the far corner of the room where he polished an apple on the seat of his trousers before munching noisily into it.

Fiona turned. 'Good morning, matron. Your patient is making satisfactory progress.'
'I am very glad indeed to hear that, nurse.' She turned to Robert. 'I had a woebegone
looking lout round our door first thing this morning asking how you were and launching
into lengthy explanations about how he had to search to find anyone in the woods to help
him.' She snorted indignantly. 'Told me you had just vanished.'

Aunt Isobel paused and looked very hard at him. 'The whole business sounds distinctly
odd to me. I find it hard to imagine you just falling in like that.'

Robert took another mouthful of egg and chewed it thoughtfully.

'I do not require a censored version,' declared Aunt Isobel sternly.

'Of course not, Aunt. I was just wondering where to begin.' This was, in fact, the
truth. Where should he begin? 'My memory is a bit vague, I guess. You know, there are
one or two gaps.'

'Most convenient I must say, Robert. Still we will leave that till later.'

'What about Tweed Jacket?' asked Robert.

'Yes, what about him?' inquired Fiona. 'How did he find you?'

'Ah yes, you mean Dr Sandy McDugall,' put in their aunt.

'A doctor?' Robert queried.

'Research. Studied conservation I believe. I've seen him around on occasions. Turns
up at Archaeological Society meetings.'

'Well, Robert?'

He looked across at his sister. 'What's that meant to mean?'

'Where did you see him? How did you meet him? How did he come to bring you home
in his car with that pretty Chinese girl?'

Benjamin, unnoticed by the others, bowed solemnly in the corner and shook hands
with himself. Aunt Isobel without turning her head said, 'Enough of that nonsense
Benjamin and hurry up and finish that apple.'

'Sis, that's enough questions to keep me busy for quite some time.'

'Come on – do tell.'

'Gee you do persist. Well Steve and I saw him with this girl – his fiancée, she is – on
the bridge just before we got to Ossian's Hall.' He felt himself grow red in the face as
he recalled his embarrassment at thinking the cave was a natural feature and not manmade.
'And . . . er . . . then at Ossian's Cave.'

Aunt Isobel never missed anything. 'I suppose you were deceived by it like most
people.' She looked at her watch. 'Time for me to do the shopping. Then I want to
develop the film I took of you the other day.' She smiled at him. 'You can get up for a
little while when you have completed your breakfast.'

When she had gone Benjamin fairly bounced out of the corner like an india-rubber
ball, his yo-yo zapping in and out, his eyes dancing.

Fiona sat on the edge of his bed.

'You can tell us now, Mac. We'll keep it a secret.'

'A thousand million secrets,' gasped Benjamin.

Robert drank the rest of his tea, ate up the last piece of toast and honey and settled
back against the pillows. 'Okay folks, here it comes, the whole works.'

He proceeded to describe the day's events as well as he could recall them. He could
not have had a more attentive audience. They sat and listened as though their lives
depended on it. Occasionally they gave an exclamation of surprise. 'Really Mac.' Or
'Fifty-two surprises and all of them Chinese.'

At last the tale was finished. There was silence in the bedroom at Arisaig. Robert
leaned back against the pillows, conscious again of the throbbing in his head as he studied

the other two. Benjamin looked more owlish than ever. 'It's better than TV any day,' he said.

'Well it certainly was exciting,' commented Fiona, a thoughtful look in her green eyes – almost as if to say 'you're holding back on us Mac.'

But he wasn't deliberately holding back any significant detail. Perhaps he had forgotten the twig that crackled behind him when he was eating his lunch and that strange feeling of being pushed. But by whom? And there again there was that moment when he had awoken and had the impression that Steve had been staring at something or someone behind him.

Fiona stood up and he knew that she was going to play at nurses again. 'Time for you, young man, to have a rest.'

'Yes nurse,' he said, grateful not to be questioned.

'Come on Numbers.'

Five thousand and twenty-five,' Benjamin said, delighted with the nickname. He turned and bowed solemnly to Robert, flicked out his yo-yo and sent it soaring up to the ceiling in a long curving arc before appearing to lose it up his sleeve. He shook hands with himself. 'Honourable Numbers bids his Big White Chief happy slumbers.'

Fiona cuffed him lightly. 'Away with you, Numbers.'

In a second he had gone and she was left staring at him.

'Aunt Isobel isn't the only one who is wondering how you came to fall in,' she remarked softly.

After lunch there was an unexpected visitor for Robert. He was sitting in the back garden reading when he heard voices and looking up saw Tweed Jacket coming out of the back door.

His voice sounded stronger today but it was still huskier than when they had met in South Street.

'Recovered from your swim?' he asked genially as Aunt Isobel retired back to the house and the dark room where she was printing the negatives she had developed that morning.

Robert was on his feet despite the pain.

'Oh gee, I am mighty grateful to you. You saved my life.'

He could not read the expression in the stranger's eyes because of the green shades but there was an underlying meaning to his words which he could not make out.

'Yes I did. Perhaps Robert – er Matheson is it?'

Robert nodded. 'Yes.'

'You will be more careful in future. I,' and there was no mistaking the emphasis on the I, 'would not like anything untoward to happen to you.'

Robert grinned. 'Me neither.'

'Good, we are agreed on that. My fiancée Cheryl will also be pleased to hear that.'

Tweed Jacket walked over to where he had been sitting and picked up the book *Trace Your Ancestors*.

He looked keenly at Robert. 'You want *Your Scottish Ancestry*, much more appropriate in your case.'

'My case,' Robert echoed, feeling weak at the knees.

'Precisely – your case. Not mine. Nor anyone else's. But yours.' He replaced the book. 'I do make myself quite clear I trust.'

Robert did not know how to react. Should he pretend he did not understand, come right into the open about it all to a perfect stranger or say absolutely nothing.

He said nothing.

'By the by, I may call you Robert?'

'Sure.'

'Good. And I am Sandy. No need for formality when a life has been at stake.'

Robert thought it unusual but again said nothing.

'I hope we shall be friends.' He smiled in such a friendly fashion that Robert found himself liking him.

'Sure Sandy. We're friends. And I hope that will include my sister Fiona. And not forgetting Benjamin my cousin.'

Again the smile. 'Good. Good.' He looked down the long tree-lined garden. 'A lovely garden Miss Matheson keeps. You must help her – when you have time.'

Robert found himself listening for the pause: it was obviously Sandy's way of emphasising something.

'I'll find time. Somehow.'

'Yes I imagine you will be busy, preoccupied. See you in the Sandeman Library one of these days. It has a fine section on local history. Could be of special interest to you, Robert.'

'I'll remember that.'

'Yes do. Well now, I must be on my way.' He ran a hand through his fair hair. 'But I'll keep in touch.'

Robert started towards the door but Tweed Jacket – he still thought of him as that – was already walking down the garden.

'Seems you have a gate. It will let me down to the North Inch.'

Tweed Jacket opened the gate and then looked hard at Robert from behind those secret green shades.

'You are creating a great deal of interest in these parts Robert – Matheson. Do take care. Won't you? No more *falling* into deep waters. You do get my meaning!'

Extract from Fiona's diary

Gee, that must have been some experience for Mac. He could have been drowned and my guess is he never fell.

I thought I'd die when I saw him at first. White and shivering with his legs twitching. He sure was in a bad way.

It was okay this morning playing nurse and all that. But I was scared. I suppose I still am. Because if Mac did not fall in then someone tried to hurt him badly. I mean it could have been murder.

Looking at that word frightens me even more. Who would want to murder Mac? Any way, why for heaven's sake? He's only a boy, and yet he's so stubborn. So someone's trying to stop him finding out something. That still doesn't add up. Not really. I mean supposing we are Kinlochys and there was some great clan centuries ago. Does that mean anything today?

Does it make him a threat to someone? Because that's what it seems like. He's a threat because of what he knows or they think he knows and because of what he may find out. Yes that's more like it.

He's searching to find out who he is – I suppose his identity in a way – and they think he is searching for something quite different. Like lost treasure. Now I just wonder . . .

Of course the truth is with all this happening I am beginning to ask myself if I've done the right thing encouraging Mac in this escapade. He takes it all so seriously. What's more so do all the other folk who seem to be mixed up in it.

I wonder now – what would Mum and Dad have thought about it all? Funny to think that they weren't Mum and Dad at all but just family friends. I mean they were and they weren't. I can't really think of them in any other way.

78

Anyway Dad said to Robert that he was a Kinlochy so perhaps he knew he would become all involved like this.
I only hope so.

Chapter 16
WHO AM I?

'**D**on't you think the time has come to tell Aunt Isobel?' Fiona asked anxiously. Robert, leaning on the parapet of Perth Bridge lost in thought about his planned visit to Central Registrar House in Edinburgh, had not taken in what she was saying.

'Tell Aunt Isobel?'

A lorry bound for Aberdeen lumbered past and Fiona's words were drowned in the roar.

'What did you say?'

'Tell Aunt Isobel the *truth*.'

Robert straightened himself, plunged his hands deep in his pockets, and studied her expression. 'Now? Today?'

Fiona clasped her hands together, a sign of nervousness.

'Why not? Is there any point in waiting?'

'No probably you're right.' He turned and they walked off down towards the Art Gallery and Museum.

'Funnily enough I was about to tell her at the Lynedoch Monument when that spaniel appeared and we all started on about getting a dog of my own.'

'I remember. You had that look about you.'

Robert smiled. 'The trouble is, sister, you know me too well.'

'Not always,' she replied softly thinking of the missing etui snd the ransacked bedroom.

'Meaning what?'

'Meaning just that, Mac. You can never know a person too well.'

He looked at the finely drawn features, the level gaze of her green eyes, and felt oddly embarrassed. It was almost as if she were reading his thoughts.

'Look let's leave it for today. Just till – ' he gulped. 'Just till I've been to Edinburgh and learned the truth.'

Traffic ground up the hill, brakes screeched and somewhere a driver honked impatiently. But Robert heard none of it. He was oblivious to everything. He turned to Fiona and when he spoke his voice was impassioned.

'I need to know the truth about myself – about us. I can't go on in this limbo-land. Are we Mathesons, Kinlochys or someone else altogether?' He clenched his fists. 'Dad was going to tell me on my birthday so it must have seemed very important to him.'

'I know how you feel, Mac. But don't – don't for pity's sake let it rule your life.'

'Wisdom from one so young,' he teased.

'Not wisdom, just common sense. And don't you forget it.'

'Okay, okay. That's enough lecturing for one day.'

'So what about tomorrow?'

'Meaning, do you go alone without me?'

Robert took her hand. 'Come on down to the river where we can talk in peace.'

They walked beside the Tay watching an oystercatcher dip and turn over the water. On the other side of the river crows flapped through the trees.

'I'm better on my own.'

Fiona looked sad but all she said was, 'And what will you tell Aunt Isobel?'

Robert rubbed his chin. 'You think that would be a problem?'

'Of course it would. She'd want to know immediately what you were up to.'

He kicked a stone disconsolately. 'I guess you're right, sister.'

'I'll tell her we're going to see the castle, Princes Street, the Scott Monument.' She laughed. 'But not the Central Registrar's Office.'

'Let that wait till I know the truth.'

After supper that evening Robert squatted down so that he could read the titles of the books on the bottom shelf of Aunt Isobel's bookcase in the living-room.

'What are you looking for?' she asked as he pulled out a tattered 1949 edition of Muirhead's *Blue Guide to Scotland* and looked up the reference to Perth Railway Station.

'Information on the railway station. One of the largest and best in Scotland with good dining and refreshment rooms, bathrooms etc. Station Hotel sixteen shillings and sixpence for bed and breakfast. What would it cost now?'

'More like twenty-five pounds. Your thirst for history is insatiable. I've never known anything like it in all my life,' said Aunt Isobel.

Fiona looked pointedly at Robert but he stubbornly refused to take the opportunity to explain why he was so obsessed with the urge to learn all he could about his new home country. 'You know I've always liked anything to do with Scotland.'

'Liked,' she laughed. 'You're absorbed in it.' She came over and stood looking at the books. 'Old family friends some of them,' she remarked.

Fiona knew immediately what she meant. 'Yes. I've books like that, but of course not nearly so many as Robert.'

'Anyway to the station. I am not an encyclopaedia, Robert, but I do happen to know that in the spring of 1848 Perth and London were finally linked by rail. And I am told – because I was not there at the time – '

Robert and Fiona laughed as indeed they were meant to do.

'That everyone from the Provost to directors of the Scottish Central Railway and the Midland Junction and Edinburgh and Northern Railways had a great day of junketing. But there was no railway station then so they ate in a wooden hut. Later, of course, they built the station you will see tomorrow and Queen Victoria herself often used the so-called refreshment rooms on her journeys to and from Balmoral.'

Robert stood up, gazing at her in amazement. 'You are an encyclopaedia you know.'

'Really you are,' chorused Fiona.

Aunt Isobel looked suitably abashed. 'Well I do know someone connected with the railways – someone interested in their history. Travels all over Scotland by rail when – ' she paused and Robert had the feeling she was going to say 'he' but for some reason preferred not to, for she continued 'when the opportunity arises'.

Later, as they went upstairs to bed, Fiona remarked, a wicked grin on her elfin features. 'I wonder if the source of all that railway knowledge is a *man* friend?'

'Someone who visits Arisaig late at night,' mused Robert, adding quietly to himself, 'and comes in via an open window from the back garden.'

Fiona would have asked him what he meant but at that moment Aunt Isobel came to the bottom of the stairs and called out, 'Hurry up you two and I will come up and say goodnight.'

And as Robert turned to acknowledge her remark Fiona took the opportunity to rush up the remaining stairs.

'Bags the bathroom first,' she called.

'Wretch,' he shouted goodnaturedly.

Robert did not normally believe in omens, good or bad, but when he woke to see a lowering grey sky and the curtains moving in the wind he had a horrible feeling that things were not going to work out. He dressed hurriedly.

'I have to know who I am. I have to know.' He kept repeating the words as if by doing so he would translate the wish into fact . . .

Perth Station was the first foreign station he had ever been in and he did not quite know what to expect. It was a fine example of Victorian architecture but very cold in the east wind.

'I want to get this over with,' he said abruptly.

'Patience, Mac.'

He grinned ruefully as they climbed aboard the train and settled down to watch the passing countryside.

'I'd sure have liked to travel in a steam engine train,' he remarked. 'You know, smoke belching out.'

'And the engine making grunting noises when it went uphill,' put in Fiona, her imagination running away with her.

Even though it was still early in the morning when they arrived in Edinburgh, Waverley Station was packed. All parking spaces were taken and a line of cars nosed its way round the station, frustrated drivers hoping to grab a space. Taxis honked impatiently and travellers bustled along, cases in hand.

For a moment the noise and movement dazed Robert. This really was quite different from Jasper. He took another look at the street map he had bought in Menzies and off they set for Waverley Bridge Street. Robert walked up the long incline from the station at such a brisk pace that Fiona found it hard to keep up.

They turned right towards Princes Street but within a few yards Fiona remembered the ten-centuries-old castle. She turned. There it loomed, a stone silhouette against the grey sky.

'Robert, look!' she cried.

He stopped and looked behind him. 'What is it?'

'The castle, don't say you'd forgotten about it.'

'Gee,' he was instantly contrite, 'I had. I guess my mind was elsewhere.'

Pedestrians jostled by as they stood gazing at it.

An American woman of ample girth and florid complexion panted to a halt and gasped to her male companion.

'Isn't that just wonderful? But really, honey, why didn't they build the castle nearer the station?'

Robert and Fiona dissolved into laughter, the spell broken. When they reached Princes Street and were waiting to cross, Robert looked along at the 200-foot-high Scott Monument which was built some one-and-a-half centuries ago. Later that morning they were to climb its 287 steps and look through the drizzling rain at the New Town.

Once across Princes Street they walked along until they came to West Register Street. Ahead of them lay great iron gates and then a fine sweep of steps leading to the offices of the Registrar for Births, Marriages and Deaths. Robert went up and read the times for the public office and search room – 9.30 a.m. to 4.30 p.m.

He looked at Fiona, feeling guilty about leaving her to stand alone in the cold and wet, but the quest was such an intensely personal thing that he wanted to make the inquiries on his own.

Fiona smiled wanly. 'It's okay Mac. On you go. I'll wait here.'

He hardly waited to say 'thank you' before he was off up the steps, through the entrance doors, past the small inquiries cubicle on the left and into the census record office for the whole of Scotland.

The thought suddenly awed him and he stood inside the doorway looking around him. It was a strange room, not at all like anything he had imagined. Round and with a high dome, its walls were lined with files stretching four storeys up. Ahead was a sign saying 'Please queue here,' and already there was a motley queue of people. Behind the long counter, men and women were busy answering questions and producing records.

With his heart hammering against his side, he took his place at the end of the queue. This was so different from the friendly informality of the Perthshire local office. He felt vulnerable, aware that others would hear his business – business that he wanted to keep private as long as possible.

When eventually a lady was free he stood momentarily transfixed with doubt and anxiety. Walking forward he gripped the edge of the counter and leaned forward. His voice was husky.

'I want help. I – I need,' he found himself almost stammering so he took a deep breath and began again. 'I am trying to trace my parents and details of my birth.'

The lady smiled kindly at him.

'That should be quite easy,' she began encouragingly. 'It is just a little difficult at times when someone asks us for information regarding a birth before 1854.'

'So you have them before that,' he exclaimed.

She nodded, then noticing the blue ancestry leaflet clutched in his hands, said, 'But you will have read all that in the leaflet. After all, we have some four thousand volumes, not all indexed by any means, covering the years 1553 to 1854. So you can imagine the problems that do turn up at times.'

He nodded. 'Yes I can.'

'But what would you like to know?'

Put like that it all sounded so delightfully simple. How he wished it were . . .

'My adopted name is Matheson, I was born in Perth fifteen years ago on 10 February, and then taken to Canada.' He paused.

'Yes,' she smiled helpfully, 'and your real name is – '

'Kinlochy,' he mumbled in a quiet voice.

'Sorry, I didn't catch the name.'

He sensed rather than saw the woman on his right leaning over, all ears, waiting to catch every word, and felt vulnerable. 'Kinlochy,' he repeated in a louder voice.

'An interesting name. Unusual too I should think.'

'Yes it is.'

'That should make it that bit easier.' She hesitated. 'There is a modest search fee of five pounds but that will cover the copy of the extract of your birth.'

Robert began to feel more hopeful. 'Oh that's okay. I have the money.'

'Well I won't be many minutes so if you would just wait there please.'

She turned and left him standing there anxious and sweating slightly. 'Oh God it must be all right. They must have the details.' He was saying the words to himself with now desperate hope and anxiety mingled in a stomach-churning cocktail.

The minutes dragged by. He scuffed his feet, peered up at the seemingly endless files of records stretching back over the years, watched the researchers behind the counter and studied the expressions on those standing by the counters. In fact, he did everything he could to keep his mind off the possible outcome of the search. So much depended on the result: his whole identity was at stake. He just had to know the name of his parents and who they were. Only then could he even start to discover the truth about his ancestors.

Finally she returned, a puzzled expression on her face. 'I am very sorry. I just cannot understand it.'

'Understand what?'

'There does not seem to be a record anywhere of that name.'

Robert's voice was hoarse with urgency. 'But there must be. There's got to be.'

She shook her head. 'I have even had a search made of the adopted children's register in case the papers were taken out in Scotland rather than Canada.'

'I certainly know of no papers in Canada.'

'Of course you could just have been adopted without legal formalities if you were taken abroad shortly after your birth.'

'I suppose so,' he said dully, hardly comprehending what she was saying. He found to his annoyance that his legs were shaking so he leaned for support against the counter.

'It's as if I don't exist,' he said.

'Nonsense, of course you exist. What is more you have a name. Matheson. A good Scottish name too.'

'But I need to know who my parents were.' His voice was rising. '*They* must have existed, had a name.'

She tried to placate him sympathetically. 'Look, there could be any number of explanations.'

Robert was prepared to seize on anything that held out even the smallest grain of hope.

'For instance you could be wrong about your birth date.'

Robert thought for a moment. 'No. I am positive about that.'

She looked disappointed. 'Oh that is unfortunate.'

Robert's mind was racing. There had to be an explanation. But what?

'What about the spelling of the name. Perhaps it was Finlochy. Yes I'll try that,' and possibly glad of an excuse to get away from his bewildered accusing eyes she hurried off.

Robert's memory of that terrible moment on the ski-slope was etched indelibly on his mind. His father's voice cut across his thoughts. 'Never forget it. You're a Kinlochy now.'

Kinlochy. Not Finlochy or Kinloch or any other number of permutations. Kinlochy. His name was Kinlochy. His father had said so.

The researcher came back unhappily twisting the chiffon scarf at her throat. 'No luck at all. I am afraid we will need further information before we can make any progress.' He noticed the subtle transfer from 'I' to 'we'. The responsibility for failing to find the details was being shared – now it belonged to the organisation and him together. She was already becoming a helpless onlooker.

Then she dispelled that impression. 'Look I am very sorry but we – ' there it was the corporate 'we' again – 'do need to know more. You do understand.'

He sensed she was appealing to him. 'Be reasonable,' she was saying. Keep a stiff upper lip. It isn't the end of the world. But it was . . .

His eyes stinging, he paid for the unsuccessful search and mumbled a hurried 'thank you' before stumbling out of the office, past the security cubicle and out through the doors into the wind and rain. He stood there for a moment shivering with the reaction from the news.

It was all so desperately unfair. He had come thousands of miles only to be told that he was not a Kinlochy and that there was not even a trace of a Kinlochy round that date.

Robert suddenly felt as if he wanted to go and hide in a corner but he could not: he had the world to face, beginning with his own sister.

He looked around for her. People scurried down the street and a multi-coloured bus drove past in Princes Street. Someone walked down the steps with high clattery heels, but Fiona was nowhere to be seen.

Anxiously he started walking towards the gates. He had been wrong to leave her there on her own. Wrong and selfish. Her safety was more important than his search.

Robert had reached the bottom step when he caught sight of the frail-looking figure huddled at the far end of the step. He rushed over to her.

'Fiona. Are you all right?'

She looked up and the elfin features were transformed by a smile of welcome and relief. 'Thank goodness you're out of that place. But what on earth happened to you, Mac? Fifty minutes you were in there.'

He took her by the arm. 'You're half-frozen. Come on and we'll get a cup of coffee and something to eat.'

'Yes that would be nice.' she stood up hurriedly and studied his expression. 'Oh Robert, I am sorry.'

She was being sympathetic but it was too much for him. He began swearing. His hand grasped her arm convulsively so that she nearly called out. She could see him squeezing his eyes together as if trying to shut out the memory or, more realistic perhaps, tears that threatened to appear.

'Fiona they don't know who I am. They've never heard of me. I've not even been born in their damned records.'

With his free hand he rubbed his eyes. 'Before Dad died he told me I was a Kinlochy.'

Fiona became aware that people were watching them. The longer she let this go on, the worse state he was going to get into.

When she spoke, her voice was firm and encouraging. 'Come on, Mac. We Kinlochys want our tea. We are not going to be defeated by any old Records Office.' She paused hopefully, studying his expression.

It seemed ages to Fiona before Robert reacted. She could see him gritting his teeth. Then he blew his nose and shook his head violently. The grin when it came was a poor lopsided affair but it was a grin all the same.

'We Kinlochys are not going to be defeated and we Kinlochys want our tea.'

Then he jammed Aunt Isobel's tartan bonnet on his head and set off down the road.

Extract from Fiona's diary

Silly stupid I am not to have seen that Robert has got himself all tangled up in this business so that it has become some sort of obsession. He's really gone over the top and then today I thought he was going to flip after he went to the Registrar General's Office in Edinburgh. He looked beaten, all white and shrivelled.

85

Then somehow he pulled himself out of it at the last moment and we went and had tea. Lukewarm and in a cracked cup it was but Mac began to regain his old determination – I wonder though if that is a good thing in the end. Perhaps it would figure out for the best if he just dropped it and got on with the business of living a normal life.

I think he feels he has lost his identity and is searching as much for himself as for his pedigree. Hope that makes sense but I understand it anyway. No one else can do it for him. I suppose I can help. But in the end it is up to him.

I suppose this is what life is all about. I mean the big tattie always rolls home. Hey that's quite good off the top of my head – big tattie I mean. Even Benjamin has got to work things out himself. He's just crazy about liquorice – Aunt Isobel calls it liquorish. He's always sucking giant sticks of it or chewing liquorice toffees.

Now that's okay by me but his dentist – and he's sure scared of him – keeps telling him that they are ruining his teeth. Benjamin was chanting away to himself tonight – an apple a day keeps the doctor away, two apples a day keep the dentist away. Hurroo hurray. It rhymes! So he scrunches his way through two of Aunt Isobel's Cox Pippins every day and then says he can eat as much liquorice as he likes.

I told him that was nonsense but he paid no attention and just started chanting again. That was silly stupid.

Chapter 17
SEAN MOIDART

Sean Moidart – Robert found the resemblance uncanny

D ejected and at a dead-end in his search, Robert was beginning to wonder if the only way to make progress was to hire one of the many private record agents in Edinburgh. They would have the expertise: they would know exactly how to go about it.

But they would be expensive, especially if the search were complicated and lengthy and it could easily be both. He pondered the problem before he went to sleep. In the morning he had made up his mind. He knew what he would have to do.

When Robert arrived down at breakfast wearing his Matheson kilt for the second time, Benjamin had already nearly finished his. He was sitting gazing into his tea-cup with such concentration that Robert wondered what he was looking at.

'Five guesses what's in my cup?'

Then Robert remembered the ritual that had developed at breakfast. Fiona, looking almost as earnest as Benjamin did, would peer into his cup and predict all sorts of exciting things which never failed to delight the younger boy.

'Not that old business again,' he remarked as he poured himself a cup of tea.

'Don't be so s-s-superior about it. Just because she doesn't read your cup for you.' Benjamin turned the cup upside down, evidently to get a better view of the tea leaves, and some tea dribbled out onto his plate.

At that moment Fiona entered the kitchen. 'Careful or you'll lose all the tea leaves.'

'You think so, Fiona?' asked Benjamin hastily righting the cup. 'Look at this,' and he passed the cup over to Fiona as if it were a piece of rare porcelain.

Fiona leaned forward, arms on the table and scrutinised it.

'Ah,' she began in a mysterious voice that had Benjamin nearly jumping out of his skin with excitement. 'I see all sorts of things. A bridge.'

'That doesn't sound awfully exciting.'

'Aah, but here there's ice-cream and something special for lunch.'

'But can't you s-see s-something more exciting?'

87

Fiona looked again. 'Well there are lots of things but I can't make them out. Oh wait a minute, here's a stranger.'

And so it went on with Fiona's inventiveness gradually running out. Finally when Robert had drunk a cup of tea himself Benjamin asked, 'Why don't you read Robert's cup?'

Robert's hand went out to the tea-pot but Benjamin was quicker and had seized the cup and handed it to Fiona. 'Please look.'

She glanced at it, trying to look serious, but there was a mischievous twitch to her mouth. Robert groaned aloud knowing she was going to make fun of him.

'An absolutely gorgeous blonde with long slim legs.'

Benjamin giggled. 'Robert's going to have a girlfriend,' he chanted. Then he made a loud scrunching sound as he bit deeply into a large red apple.

Fiona looked at Benjamin. 'He's had lots of girlfriends already.'

'Oh cut it out, Fiona,' he said, feeling rather foolish.

Fiona's eyes were serious, speculative. 'You have got a funny cup to read.'

'Not another blonde,' he groaned.

'No a b-brunette,' said Benjamin. 'Two girlfriends in one day.'

Fiona was still looking serious. 'Not two girlfriends. Two men.' She turned the cup at an angle to see better. 'Yes Mac, definitely two men and one of them seems to be chasing you.'

The words made him feel apprehensive. Abruptly he got to his feet. 'I think I'll go and chase the sun on the North Inch.'

An hour later he returned and had hardly opened the front door when something zapped out at him. He halted in alarm.

'A million laughs, ha ha ha.' And Benjamin, obviously delighted to see him, zipped his yo-yo in the air in an extravagant parabola.

'Gee you took me by surprise.'

'Sorry Rob – I mean Robert. Fiona says I've only to call you Rob if you're in danger.' His yo-yo had vanished into a pocket; he pushed his glasses up the bridge of his nose with a forefinger and looked owlish. 'Fiona says I've got something which will interest you.'

'Okay let's see, but I can't think what it could be.'

Benjamin went across to the old dresser by the grandfather clock and lifted a single sheet of green paper. Robert glanced casually at it.

'Sean Moidart invites you to attend a lecture on "Your Scottish Ancestry" in the Assembly Hall on 1 July at eight o'clock. By invitation only. Bring this notice with you. Refreshments – 9.30 p.m. By courtesy of the History of Scotland Association.'

Robert stood studying the flimsy sheet of paper, unaware it would affect his whole future.

The coincidence was uncanny. This must be yet another example of Fiona's gift of second sight. Her green eyes were grave.

'But it was just something I saw in those old tea leaves,' she protested. 'Nothing more.' Robert remained unconvinced.

'After all, Mac, I've been reading cups for several mornings now and nothing has happened before.'

'But this,' pointed out Robert, 'was the first time you've read mine. And you've been right about me in other ways in the past.'

'You mean when you were buried in the snow.'

He nodded. 'Exactly.' He walked across to the cabinet in the living-room and stared at the empty spot where the beautiful etui had stood. 'There's something I've never told you.'

'Oh.' She looked up from the lightning sketch she was making of him on the back of Sean Moidart's notice. 'And what was that?'

'It was when I was skiing down Shangri La. I heard your voice as clear as anything in my head.'

'Yes Mac, I wondered if you did.'

'Do you remember what you were shouting to me?'

Fiona pushed a strand of fair hair back from her forehead and sucked the end of her pencil pensively. 'Yes,' she said at last. 'Rob, turn south.'

'Those words saved my life. I suppose it was the "Rob" that alerted me. A small crevasse was ahead of me. Perhaps three or four yards. That was all.'

Fiona sat looking at him. 'Sometimes it frightens me, Robert. This seeing into the future. I wish it didn't happen.'

Robert looked at the notice. 'This will be one of the men in the tea leaves.'

'Yes,' she spoke quickly. 'You will see him tonight. I know you will.'

'But what on earth do I say to Aunt Isobel?'

'I don't know. But you will see him.'

'She's bound to smell a rat.'

'Not if she doesn't know, Mac.'

'Don't talk in riddles, Fiona.'

'I didn't mean to – really I didn't. But I know you are going to see Sean Moidart.' She started doodling in a corner of the notice – a tall, commanding figure, dark with a jutting nose, wearing a kilt.

'And who's that meant to be?'

'That,' she replied in a whisper, 'is the man you are going to meet tonight.'

As Robert sat down in the sparsely-filled hall he got the shock of his life. There striding across to the rostrum was the man Fiona had drawn. The chairman introduced him as Sean Moidart, one of Scotland's leading authorities on conservation and Scottish history. The tartan looked vaguely familiar but Robert could not place the dark greens and blues with the thin lines of red.

He could still hardly believe his luck. A phone call had come at supper. Robert had answered it and a precise lady's voice, a Mrs Adele Bredie, had asked for Miss Matheson. 'It is to do with the Famine Appeal Fund collection,' she had said.

A brief conversation had ensued with Aunt Isobel, who had then announced she was going out to a meeting that night. Fiona had looked across at Robert and winked. So he had said nothing and here he was at the lecture and there standing large as life in front of him was the man in Fiona's sketch.

Uncanny was the only word for it.

Sean Moidart had the deepest, most resonant voice Robert had ever heard and what he had to say held him spellbound for well over an hour. True he knew a certain amount of it already but there were valuable points to follow. For instance, there was the Scots Ancestry Research Society and the Scottish Genealogy Society who could be consulted. Kirk Session Records, he learned, would give details of people leaving the parish. Newspaper files could prove invaluable: the *Perthshire Advertiser*'s files, for example, went back to 1837, and then there were all the books written since the 1700s, including the first two Statistical Accounts of Scotland. Wills and details of house sales . . .

It was during the ensuing question and answer session that Robert began to feel he was being watched. The urge to look round was almost irresistible.

The feeling left him abruptly. At the same moment a strange harsh whisper of a voice that had the power to carry the length of the hall asked a question.

'How would the speaker begin his searches for a name of which the Registrar's Office could find absolutely no trace?'

Robert felt as if someone had hit him in the stomach.

The Chairman, a reverend gentleman whose name Robert had missed, remarked archly, 'Like one of Edward Lear's delightful concoctions.'

The man with the strange voice retorted, 'I did not exactly have something like that in mind. But nevertheless . . . ' The voice trailed off into silence.

'Ah well,' remarked the Chairman, 'there's a poser for you Dr Moidart.'

'On the contrary, Chairman, that becomes a challenge which we can either accept or refuse.' His gaze swept the audience in such a penetrating way that Robert could have sworn that he had looked specially at him. 'No man – nor woman for that matter,' there was a faint laugh from the audience, but he quelled it with a gesture, 'has lived in Scotland without leaving an imprint, however faint, on the sands of time. His marks will still be there for you to trace.'

With these words still ringing in his ears Robert later enjoyed a cup of tea and an egg sandwich, while all about him people gathered in small groups, chatting animatedly. During the end of the question session Robert had glanced quickly behind him to see if he could spot who had asked that disturbing question: but with no success. Now he moved unobtrusively from group to group, studying faces. Absorbed in his search, he nearly knocked into Sean Moidart. He stopped, slopping some of his tea and began to apologise.

But the rumbling voice halted him. 'No need to young man.'

Robert looked up. The tall Highlander had obviously known that he was about to apologise. He was smiling – a friendly yet serious smile. 'So you have come.'

Robert was puzzled. 'Yes. I wanted to. I had to.'

Sean Moidart towered above him and when they got round to shaking hands he felt as if a wave of power had swept through his being. His handshake gave the impression of immense strength but it was not one of those hearty, man-to-man crushing handshakes that some of the Canadian park rangers affected. This was a different kind of power – something at once more elemental and more controlled.

'So you are searching for your pedigree.'

'Yes. But how did you know?'

The big man smiled disarmingly. 'Well now you would hardly be here otherwise.' He stood looking down at him, almost as if he were looking at an old friend from the past.

At that moment the Chairman appeared. 'A most entertaining and instructive talk if I may say so Dr Moidart.'

'Thank you. I enjoyed it myself.'

The Chairman laughed at his remark, introduced him briefly to a Mrs Adele Bredie, a plain-looking woman with a flat cold gaze who asked an obvious question about tracing a lost relative. Sean Moidart answered her with grave Highland courtesy and, after a long curious look at Robert, she had slipped away. Was it just a coincidence, or could she be the lady of the same name who had phoned earlier?

'Yes everything comes back to us eventually – the knowledge of past lives and experiences.' The kilted figure seemed to be answering a comment from a small portly man who had joined them but Robert knew that the comment was directed at him. He had the odd feeling that Sean Moidart was speaking on two levels at once.

Sean Moidart let his gaze sweep round the emptying hall. His deepset eyes seemed to focus suddenly and, half turning, Robert spotted Mrs Bredie, lips pursed, eyes filled with suspicion, watching them . . .

'Aye you're going to need to be careful who you talk to and what you say,' he paused. 'But trust will never be a problem between us two.'

And knowing that it wouldn't be, Robert blurted out, 'I am trying to find my real parents. My real name – '

'Of course you are.' The big man spoke in such a matter-of-fact tone that Robert almost missed the implication – simply that he knew that already.

'When my father was about to die he told me I was a –'

His companion silenced him with a gesture. 'Keep that name to yourself.' It was almost as if Robert had said 'Kinlochy' aloud. 'There are folk in these parts who already believe they know your true name and why you are here.' His voice deepened. 'You have a long, lonely, deep furrow to plough. You will need all your courage and determination – aye and much more if you are to succeed.'

Robert leaned forward. 'I must succeed.'

In that case Robert, you're searching for more than a name and a clan. You are searching for the heritage that has been awaiting you for centuries.'

'For centuries,' Robert broke in. 'What do you mean?'

'Don't interrupt.' He was stern and forbidding. 'We have little time together though I shall be there in the long term future when you need me. You are also searching for your own personal identity. You have first to come to terms with yourself, as everyone else in the world has to.'

He paused and when he resumed he spoke more slowly to emphasise his words. 'Until you have done that you can accomplish nothing of value.'

'Now you really mustn't take up all the speaker's time, young man.' It was the Chairman speaking.

Robert began to mutter apologies.

'I will be only a moment,' the tall Highlander was saying as the Chairman turned to answer a remark from a bystander.

Sean Moidart put out his hand. 'Good luck, Robert – ' He did not actually say 'Kinlochy' but again Robert heard the name in his mind and in the deep voice of the other man.

'And be careful – very careful – who you trust.'

'Sure I'll take care. And thanks Dr Moidart.'

In that moment Robert decided he would tell Benjamin that very evening. As it turned out, Benjamin was to take the news with enormous gravity and Robert felt that the young boy would prove a valuable ally, but even as he was making this decision Sean Moidart was moving away to join the Chairman for what the latter described as 'a wee dram down the road'.

Abruptly he turned back to him. 'Take great care on the way home. Keep to the main roads. Take no shortcuts. Stop and speak to no one.' His voice dropped. 'And beware of the Whisperer. He is your enemy. He always has been and he always will be.'

Then he was gone and Robert was left standing alone in a corner of the hall, a half-drunk cup of tea in his hand. The hall was nearly empty and through the open door he could see it was already growing dark outside.

Dark with wisps of trailing mist.

He hurried out into the night and, almost at once, cold damp tendrils of grey wreathed round him.

Street lights flickered eerily. The sound of traffic was dulled, distant. He paused to get his bearings and recalled the narrow winding vennel which would save him time. He came upon the opening in less than a minute and turned down between high walls that seemed to press in on him.

Robert had taken only a few steps when he remembered Sean Moidart's warning. 'Keep to the main roads. Take no shortcuts,' and already he had disobeyed him.

It was then that he heard the footsteps behind him and a faint padding sound. Then an evil chuckle like the gurgle of a sewer followed by silence again which was broken only by the sound of his own footsteps.

This was madness. He should have stayed on the main road, but now it was too late and fear like ice particles from the freezer slithered down his back.

Another grotesque gurgle came from behind him. He felt as if someone was breathing down his neck. He turned the corner ahead. A solitary street lamp illuminated coils of mist drifting towards him. As he drew level with the lamp the mist thickened. In a blind moment of panic Robert turned and saw looming up behind him a vague amorphous figure, hands stretched out to clutch his throat.

The voice was harsh like dead leaves skittering across the pavement. 'Wait for me, my pretty boy.'

The figure pounced.

The bulb in the lamp flickered eerily . . . and went out.

Robert ducked instinctively and he felt a rasping inrush of breath as that awful figure slithered past him.

Total darkness. Silence. The thudding of his heart echoed against his side and a padding sound of feet was coming towards him.

Robert turned and ran back the way he had come. All the way along that narrow winding vennel it was dark and damp and frightening: all the lamps were extinguished. So he ran blindly, crying out in his mind for help but not daring to shout aloud.

His right hand brushed against the stone side of a wall reminding him that there was a corner. He veered slightly to the left and there ahead of him were the lights on the main road, a car cruising slowly by, people walking on the pavement. The breathing and the padding behind him grew louder, more insistent. He spurted forward and in seconds was on the pavement and turning to the left in the direction of home. Behind him the breathing and the padding had stopped.

But Robert did not stop running till several minutes had passed. Nor did his heart stop pounding until he had reached his front door and the safety of Arisaig . . .

Chapter 18
SURPRISE
ENCOUNTER

Two hands shot out and seized Robert,
choking back his cry for help

Danger was lurking in the deep shadows of Arisaig. Thick swathes of mist curled up from the North Inch. Less than thirty feet away outside the front gate, the street lamp cast a yellow pool of light on the pavement. As it reached the roses in the garden it grew diffuse and the silken petals took on a ghostly pallor. The stench of the fog was rough and suffocating in Robert's mouth. He felt it settle deeper on his hair and face making him want to tear it away as if it were a mosaic of giant cobwebs each intent on wrapping itself round him.

Robert, his heart still pounding against his side, put his hand in his pocket to find the house key. Then he remembered. He had left it on the hall table when he had gone out.

For no reason panic threatened to engulf him. Urgently he turned and peered across the road. Was that a figure lurking on the opposite pavement or merely a thickening of the fog? He strained his eyes. There was a movement, a scraping of feet on the tarmac . . .

Robert shivered more from fear than cold. He stabbed a finger on the doorbell, heard it echo eerily through the old house, waited for the welcome sound of footsteps on the hall floor.

It was then that danger took the shape and form of a large threatening figure in a heavy raincoat and hat who slid out from the dark shadows of the house to loom over Robert. He started in surprise, just managing to stifle a cry.

A hand clamped itself down on his shoulder almost forcing him to his knees. Desperately Robert tried to wriggle free. Powerful fingers settled round his throat. The pressure tightened.

It was then that he heard footsteps approaching along the pavement. He opened his mouth to call for help. A second hand jerked across his mouth and drew him back against the stranger. He squirmed from one side to another but all in vain. The stranger's hands were immensely powerful. Finally he relaxed his body, hoping his adversary would loosen his hold on him, but the man was not deceived and, if anything, tightened his grip.

A lean hawklike figure loomed up out of the mist at the end of the garden. Momentarily the fog cleared and the street lamp caught him in a pool of light. In that instant Robert could see the figure quite clearly.

The shock was so great that he felt as though ice had been poured into his veins. There, only feet away, was none other than the man who had chased him down the vennel.

The Whisperer was remorselessly pursuing him. So Sean Moidart had been right – this was his arch enemy. And in some curious way Robert felt that he was not just an enemy but *the* enemy and he had come from somewhere deep in his past. It was as if they were ancient protagonists. It was a fanciful thought but Fiona would have understood it.

Now the Whisperer was peering about him, his eyes scorching the eddying mist and darkness. Robert could see the long thin nose and pointed ears. Slowly the head with its sleeked down back hair began to turn towards Arisaig. Now the face looked like cracked parchment. In his mind he could hear the strange rasping voice like the hiss of a snake.

The faintest hint of a breeze that had sent the fog swirling away died abruptly. The fog, thicker and darker than ever, settled on the garden like a blanket giving him protection from those probing eyes. Robert was clenching his fists so tightly that his nails were driven sharply into the palms of his hands. He gritted his teeth and wondered why the stranger did not call out to the Whisperer because he was sure they must be working together. Then, as the figure in the fog began to move forward again, his footsteps muffled, his head bent forward, Robert began to think that perhaps the man who had such a cruel grip on him might not be on the side of the Whisperer after all.

In that case, who was he and what did he want with Robert? Surely not yet another enemy to reckon with? The thought filled him with despair. Again he tried to wrench himself free but without success. His captor was evidently as wily as he was strong.

What had happened to Fiona and Benjamin? Why had they not come to answer the bell for surely they would realise it was him? Or had someone else already infiltrated the house and even now was holding them captive? Fresh anguish overcame him. He had no right to involve them in the dangerous game he was playing.

The Whisperer's footsteps died away and the street was still. Even the swirling fog seemed to have settled down on the road and houses so that the outlines of roofs and chimney pots were blurred and insubstantial. It was like a fantasy world without roots in reality. It filled him with dread.

Gradually the stranger's grasp slackened.

The voice when it spoke was as familiar as it was unexpected.

'Verra strange it is to be sure, finding you out alone like this in the fog.'

Sergeant Wallace Ochilston paused and Robert could visualise those shrewd assessing eyes looking at him. 'You dinna know who might be out on the prowl on a night like this.'

The big policeman slowly took his hand away from his mouth. 'Now none of your shouting for help or you'll be in trouble up to your eyeballs.'

Robert stretched his neck to and fro to ease the pain. Then he nodded and, careful not to anger the policeman, he turned towards him. The dark bulk of the man stood four-square on the garden path. His eyes were in the shadow of his hat. His hands were slightly outstretched ready to seize hold of Robert if he gave the slightest indication of trying to escape.

Robert spoke quietly in case the Whisperer should be lurking behind the wall in front of the neighbouring house.

'What are you doing here?'

'Ever asking questions aren't you laddie? Will you never learn it's my job to ask the questions?'

Robert said nothing; just waited to see what Sergeant Ochilston would say next.

'As it happens I was waiting for you, Robert Matheson.'

'Why?'

'Oh I just like to ken what you're up to.' The face was inscrutable in the grey light. 'You see you're a great one for getting into mischief. I wouldn't be wanting anything else to happen on my patch. I mean that etui business was bad enough without anything else untoward occurring – if you get my meaning.'

Robert was angry. 'You'll never give me a break will you?'

'Oh I wouldn't say that laddie.'

'I would.'

'Stop getting het up and listen to me for a moment.'

Robert ground his teeth but remained silent. The dampness from the fog seemed to have penetrated his very bones and he found himself shivering again. Determinedly he tried to stop: the last thing he wanted was to have this bullying policeman think he was afraid.

A thought occurred to him. 'Why did you stop me calling out?'

'Now I wouldn't be wanting you to wake the neighbours on a night like this, would I?'

But Robert was determined to follow his line of thought through to the end. 'Was it because of the Whis – ' He choked back the rest of the name. 'That man.'

Sergeant Ochilston managed to sound incredulous. 'What man? When? That's a verra strange thing to say.'

It was Robert's turn to sound incredulous. 'That man on the pavement.'

Sergeant Ochilston took a few paces forward in his heavy fashion and appeared to peer into the fog. 'I canna see a single soul, laddie. You're havering that's what you are. Just havering.'

Robert was furious. 'You're just pretending. He was there a moment ago. On the pavement. I saw him with my own eyes.'

'It's a softening of the brain cells that you're suffering from. A damned shame really.' The sergeant appeared to be studying him carefully. 'I thought you had more brains, laddie. I'm disappointed in you, I am.'

Robert was about to exclaim in anger when it began to dawn on him that there must be a reason behind the sergeant's remarks. Either he, Robert, had imagined the suspicious-looking figure on the pavement or Sergeant Ochilston, for his own private reasons, did not want to acknowledge that he might know who the man was or what he was doing.

Robert, looking at him, wished the fog would clear so he could read his expression. Still the fog had saved him in the end, though if he had only obeyed Sean Moidart's warning he would not have been nearly trapped in the vennel by the Whisperer.

'The fog makes you imagine things,' he said at last in a dull voice.

'That's better, laddie,' exclaimed the bulky policeman more cheerfully. 'Much better. You'll learn yet who you can trust and who you can't. It takes time but you'll get there if you don't wind up in the river one of these days.'

'Wind up in the river,' declared Robert anxiously.

'Oh, just a manner of speaking,' replied the other. 'But you'll want to have eyes in the back of your head if you're going to survive.'

There was an ominous tone in the big man's voice which worried Robert. After all, that was the second warning he had received in one evening. More than anything it meant that he either possessed some very important piece of information or something of inestimable value that his enemies were determined to get. Again it reminded him of the danger to Fiona and even Benjamin. The responsibility, he felt, was almost too great to bear on his own but there was no one he could share it with, unless, yes just possibly sometime in the future, he could contact Sean Moidart.

But in the meantime it was up to him and him alone. The battle was on. As for Sergeant Ochilston, what was his role in all this? Why had he been so anxious that the Whisperer did not see Robert? For that matter perhaps he, Sergeant Ochilston, had not wanted to be seen at Arisaig either. Now there was a new dimension of concern . . .

'You're looking thoughtful, laddie,' remarked the Sergeant quietly. 'Nothing troubling you I trust.'

Robert shook his head. 'Just reckoning.'

The other rubbed his gloved hands together. 'It's getting chilly here. So I'll keep it short.'

'Should we not go inside then?'

Sergeant Ochilston appeared to consider the suggestion.

'No,' he replied at last. 'What I've got to say to you is for your ears alone.'

Robert felt a prick of fear run down his back. It sounded suspiciously as if the big policeman did not want any witnesses to their conversation.

And that, thought Robert, was hardly reassuring. He shoved his hands in his pockets, straddled his legs and prepared to listen.

'I'm going away for a wee while,' began Sergeant Ochilston. 'A spot of unexpected leave you might call it.'

'But why tell me?' asked Robert, feeling mystified.

'Aye it occurred to me you might be asking that.' He paused heavily. 'Just let's say I'm taking an interest in you, Robert Matheson. There's the wee matter of an unexplained burglary at Arisaig. Aye and the fact that your room was the only one that was ransacked. Now I'm asking myself why that should be. I think it verra strange indeed. It needs a bit of explaining, don't you think?'

Robert shrugged. 'But we've been over all this before.'

'So we have. But I believe it's persistence that counts in solving crimes.'

Somehow Robert had not thought of the word *crime* as such. It made it all sound even more serious if that were possible.

The fog was beginning to lift slightly almost as if the immediate danger facing him was over for the moment. For the first time the hum of traffic at the end of the road came clearly to him. No longer did he feel marooned in an oasis of time and mist with the policeman. Normality was surely returning at last.

But Sergeant Ochilston soon dispelled that feeling of relief. 'Now just get this straight, young Matheson. I may be going away, but you'll be watched like a hawk. Just step out of line for a moment and you'll be in deep trouble, laddie.'

Robert bit his lip but said nothing. He was determined not to be intimidated by anyone – well at least he would make sure that no one knew how he felt . . .

The sergeant had paused for a while. 'I'll say this for you, Robert Matheson. You've got guts. And there's not enough lads around these days with guts.' His tone changed abruptly as if he had not meant to let his true feelings show. 'Anyway, as I was about to say. This is a warning – a mighty serious one at that. You ignore it, lad, at your peril. Make no mistake about it. You've attracted a lot of attention since you came onto this patch. And not the right kind of attention either. So just watch it. Because as sure as a Panda's waiting down the next road for me, so trouble is waiting for you.'

He stared solidly at Robert for a full ten seconds and then without another word turned on the heels of his size ten shoes and clumped off down the path. He opened and closed the gate silently, looked carefully to right and left and then strode off into the thinning mist.

Extract from Fiona's diary

DESTINY is one of those words that always seems to me to need CAPITALS. Like a person, a very important person. Anyway I think DESTINY is taking a hand because Mac met the strangest man. Sean Moidart he's called, and the oddest thing about it is that I saw it all in Mac's tea-cup.

And I even drew him – hooked nose, dark countenance – sounds like a historical novel that. But countenance is the right word.

When I had drawn him I had the strangest feeling: I felt I was drawing someone I had known from way back ages and ages ago. He just sort of appeared on the paper before me. Wearing a kilt and yes – strangest of all – I heard the rumble of his voice in my mind. And I mean rumble. No words, just a deep rumble of a voice.

Oh yes, and I saw in the cup another figure – a man chasing Mac down a narrow sort of alleyway.

When he got in tonight I couldn't get much out of him. He was all clammed up. But he muttered something about being pursued by the WHISPERER. That gives me the heeby jeebies. And he said he bumped into Sergeant Ochilston outside the house. Now that is odd.

But DESTINY sure looks to be taking a hand. It reminds me of dear old Omar Khayyam and those lines:

> *Tis all a chequer board of nights and days*
> *Where DESTINY with men for pieces plays.*

Chapter 19
ON THEIR OWN

But even as they waved goodbye to Aunt Isobel, a figure lurked in the shadows

L ater that night the fog lifted and the stars came out. But, unknown to Robert, the real danger was only about to begin: his gravest fears were soon to be tragically realised.

He lay in bed mentally exhausted, his thoughts whirling round. Time and again he went over the events of the previous evening. Always he returned to the conundrum: what was Sergeant Ochilston up to? When his footsteps had finally died away and Robert fancied he could hear the Panda starting up and driving off he had rung the bell repeatedly.

After what had seemed like ages Fiona had come to the door. Full of apologies she had explained that she had been teaching Benjy chess and that the transistor was full on, so she had not heard the bell.

Disgruntled, Robert had pushed past her with only a cursory explanation as to what had happened. He had not wanted to alarm her. Now lying in bed he wondered what steps he could take to ensure that nothing happened to her or to Benjamin.

Eventually he fell asleep before he had reached any conclusions. But even if he had not he was already too late to prevent the sinister course of events organised by the Whisperer. In fact everything happened so quickly that he was caught unawares.

First, Aunt Isobel received a phone call shortly after breakfast from her old photographic friend Rosemary Tubble in Oban saying she had been struck by some virus which had left her so dizzy she could hardly stand up. The doctor had said it would last only a day or two but unfortunately her neighbours were away on holiday.

She did not get a chance to say another word before Aunt Isobel was promising to come over right away. After all, hadn't she, Rosemary, done the same for her earlier that very spring when she had suffered from a bad bout of 'flu.

She seemed almost apologetic when she told them. 'I simply must help my friend,' she announced a little abruptly, possibly because she was concerned about leaving the three of them alone at Arisaig. 'Now you will be all right.' She said it in a tone of voice that suggested she was trying to convince herself more than them.

98

'If you want anything you can always ring Ena McLarnty.'

'But,' put in Fiona, 'I thought you didn't like her.'

Aunt Isobel sniffed. 'I never said that. All the same, these are exceptional circumstances as I'm sure you'll realise.' She looked firmly at Robert. 'Whatever you may think of Sergeant Ochilston, he's a good man. Any more unpleasantness and you can always contact him.'

Robert, who had been trying to help Fiona work out a problem on her pocket chess-set in the living-room, recalled that the sergeant was going away on leave.

'But he won't be – ' he had been about to say 'here' but stopped himself just in time. Aunt Isobel looked puzzled. 'He won't be what?'

Embarrassed, Robert shrugged his shoulders. 'What I was going to say was he won't always be around.'

'There's no need,' declared Aunt Isobel firmly, 'to try and create problems.'

Robert, about to protest that this was not his intention, decided to say nothing.

So it was that within the hour Aunt Isobel was at the wheel of Bronco while Robert manfully swung the starter handle. There was the usual accompanying cough and splutter followed by the uneven chugging sound of the engine as it began to warm up.

The three of them stood at the gate waving her goodbye. Aunt Isobel regarded them anxiously for a moment and then juggled with the strangely shaped gear lever. Bronco gave a sudden lurch forward and then it was off with thick smoke belching out from the exhaust. All three of them turned simultaneously to watch the ancient Citroen's jerky progress down the street and were therefore unaware of the furtive figure at the other corner of the road. He stood well back in the shadow of the high wall and his eyes gleamed with malicious satisfaction as he saw their aunt leave.

The first stage in his evil plan was right on schedule. His eyes fastened greedily on the slender figure of Fiona and lingered for a moment as he thought of the next step.

*****

Fiona was the first to turn away and walk slowly back up the path towards the front door. The sun was already high in the sky and her slim shadow was cruelly foreshortened. She looked and felt vulnerable.

'We are all alone,' she remarked at last as Robert and Benjamin joined her on the doorstep.

Benjamin regarded them curiously for a moment and then laughed. 'But think of all the f-f-fun we'll have,' he declared. 'I can stay up as late as I like.' And he danced a cheerful little jig.

Robert was rueful. 'Numbers – you go to bed when you're told.' He turned to Fiona and spoke quietly. 'I know what you mean, Sis. But don't worry I'll take care.'

Benjamin looked curiously at them from behind his thick lensed glasses.

His voice was solemn with self-importance. 'I am going to work on my c-c-computer for a while,' he announced, disappearing inside the hall.

Robert carefully closed the door behind him and began to make his way towards the living-room.

'What's on your mind, Mac?'

He glared with unseeing eyes at the cabinet and the empty space formerly occupied by the etui. 'Too much. That etui thing. I'm sure there's more to it than we realise.'

Fiona's green eyes glazed over as if she were in a trance. 'We won't know the answer to that for a while.'

'What makes you think that?'

She tugged at a strand of fair hair, twisting the ends round a finger. 'I don't know, Mac. We'll just have to wait.'

'That's all we seem to be doing now,' he retorted savagely. 'Waiting. And for what. Hell, if only I could just see the name Kinlochy written down somewhere. So far I've only heard it all mixed up with the roar of the avalanche.'

He scuffed the carpet with his foot. 'Supposing it was just my imagination.' He turned to his sister. 'I need to see it written down.'

Fiona saw anguish in his face and even in the taut way he held himself. 'Mac, you didn't imagine it. And anyway what about the napkin rings? Surely that's some sort of proof.'

Robert shook his head. 'I can't explain it, Sis. I need something else, something . . .' he paused, searching for the word. 'Corroborative evidence. That's what I need.'

Fiona smiled teasingly. 'You sound like Sergeant Ochilston at his most severe.'

At that moment a small figure quietly entered the room. His eyes were thoughtful but brother and sister saw only the cherubic smile on his face.

Fiona asked him. 'Where did you spring from you old jack-in-a-box?'

Benjy, deliberately playing the fool, jumped up and down.

'Jack-in-a-b-box Numbers wants his computer manual.' Then he walked over the window seat and picked up the heavy ring-bound manual.

When he left Robert turned towards Fiona. 'I wonder how much he heard?'

She looked reprovingly at him. 'You're becoming too suspicious for your own peace of mind.'

He shrugged. 'Maybe, but we can't be too careful.' Then he changed the subject so as not to worry her.

'It strikes me Sis that our young cousin is far more astute than people give him credit for.'

'You mean he hides behind this pretence of being just a young lad.'

'Just that.'

'If you ask me, Mac, it's the result of being teased so much at school. He plays the ass and makes them laugh so in the end he's a kind of hero in his own eyes.'

Robert nodded sadly. 'I reckon you've hit the button there.' A light breeze blew the curtain back from the open window. Was it his imagination or was there a figure at the corner standing in the shadow of the wall? He stepped quickly forward, narrowing his eyes against the sunshine. But there was no one there.

Only Fiona, with a catch of her breath, noted the elongated shadow stretching out at an angle from the wall.

'I think I'll take a look at the back room,' he announced too casually to deceive his sister.

Fiona looked at him sharply. 'You mean you want to see if she's left the window open?'

Robert was taken aback. 'Something like that,' he mumbled.

Fiona's glance was steady. 'Aunt Isobel was in a right old hurry today. She wouldn't remember to close the window. Not unless it was very important.'

'And very deliberate,' he put in.

Without another word the two of them walked apprehensively into the hall and then paused as if by mutual agreement outside the back room door. They looked silently at each other.

The voice that called out in the silence of the old house might have been childish but it had a surprising authority to it.

'There's no need to go in there.'

100

They looked up the narrow curving staircase with the light filtering through the stained glass window halfway up. Benjamin was standing very still watching them.

'I've b-been in there,' he declared. 'And the w-window,' now they could detect the excitement in his voice, 'w-window was,' he stopped in mid-sentence and walked halfway down the stairs.

'Yes?' demanded Robert, unable to bear the suspense.

'Sh-Shut.'

The word seemed to float down to them syllable by syllable.

Fiona looked at Robert. 'So it was left open deliberately before.'

He nodded grimly. 'So that whoever smoked that pipe could get in and out without being seen.'

Benjamin joined them. 'And she hadn't time to warn him not to come.'

'So,' added Robert obeying an absurd desire to get the last word in, 'he won't be able to get into Arisaig and he'll know she's away.'

But it was Fiona who had the last word as it happened. 'Yes, Mac. And know that we three are on our own.'

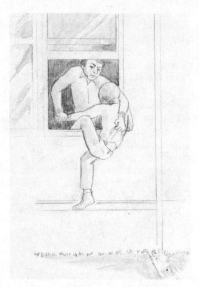

Chapter 20
UNDER SIEGE

He hauled him roughly through the open window

Robert tried to shrug it off but privately he had to admit that he was worried. He could see no immediate threat to them so long as they kept their heads. All the same it seemed too much of a coincidence to ignore.

It was Benjamin who used the phrase first. Then it was taken up by Fiona in one of her more dramatic moments.

'We're under siege,' declared the young lad excitedly.

Robert was edgy and snapped back at him. 'What do you mean?'

Benjamin looked upset. 'I was back at my computer – you know how it s-sits in my bedroom window.'

'Yes?' interrupted Robert.

'Well I l-looked up and there was the Weasel standing in the back lane staring up at me.'

Robert, who had been about to ask Fiona what she was going to do for lunch, tried to make light of it so as not to worry her.

'Just imagination, Numbers. Probably wanted to see if you would go out and play with him.'

But Benjamin shook his head. 'His eyes were all starey – you know how he looks, and he had on his headphones and, Robert, he was talking. As if giving instructions to someone.'

'Really, Benjamin. Who could the Weasel be instructing? He's only a harmless kid.'

Fiona looked at him hard. 'Since when have you thought that Rob? He's as dangerous as a snake and you know it.'

Robert was abashed. 'Okay, Sis. He's dangerous. But don't let's allow our imaginations to run away with us.'

Benjamin was watching him closely. 'There's m-more to tell.'

'Oh heck, what does that mean?' Robert asked in exasperation.

'L-Look out of the front window.'

Robert walked quickly across the living-room and pushed the window further open so that he could get a better view of the road. A cyclist was passing and an old man with a stick was hobbling along the opposite pavement. It all looked pretty innocent.

Then he saw him. Steve himself. Tall, bulky, slouching Steve, his hands in his pockets, looking suspicious as hell.

'I'd reckoned without him,' remarked Robert quietly. 'Sorry Benjy. I guess you were right after all.'

'So we are under siege,' began Fiona tremulously.

Sudden, blinding anger raged through Robert's being. He was not going to be *intimidated* by any of these goofs.

'I'm going out there to find out what the hell's happening,' he declared. He turned to Fiona. 'Don't move out of this house, Sis, not for one second.'

Benjamin zipped his yo-yo viciously to and fro. The scowl on his chubby features deepened. But there was a quiver round his lips when he announced, 'And I'm g-going round to the back of the house to s-see the W-Weasel.' The words came out slower than usual.

Robert looked at the younger lad, and felt admiration for him. But he could not allow him out there alone with the Weasel of all people. It just would not be fair. He looked at Benjamin and shook his head.

'As Fiona said, he's dangerous.'

Benjamin bit his underlip. 'You d-don't think I c-can deal with him.'

In a moment of intuition Robert knew that Benjamin had decided he had to go out there on his own. It was something he felt he just had to do. He knew how he regarded his own quest so he could understand – and sympathise.

He stepped forward and put his hand on the young lad's shoulder. 'No, I'm sure you can, Numbers. But just take care.'

Fiona looked at him doubtfully but Benjamin's eyes shone. 'You c-can rely on me, Robert.' And with that he scampered off towards the back door.

Robert turned to Fiona. 'You'd better lock it behind him. And remember, Sis, you let no one in unless it's one of us.'

She walked with him to the front door, locking it behind him. Robert braced his shoulders and began to walk smartly down the path towards the gate. He glanced up the road. The cyclist was turning the far corner. Coming slowly towards him was a small, innocuous-looking van. He paid no more attention to it and was soon walking in the direction of the North Inch.

In the distance not far from the river he could see the old man with the stick hobbling along. No danger there. But where was Steve? He could not have disappeared just like that, which meant he must be behind the high wall at the corner of the opposite pavement. He began to hurry across the road wondering if perhaps he was not being just a bit foolish about it all. Since when did the two McLarnty brothers constitute a siege? It was all very well for a youngster like Benjamin to talk in such terms but at his age he should not be taking it seriously.

He slowed to a more leisurely pace and on reaching the corner casually looked in the direction of the town. A hundred yards away Steve was sauntering along smoking a cigarette. Occasionally he kicked a stone in front of him on the path. Now Robert felt ridiculous. He had allowed himself to overreact to a non-existent situation. He began to follow the older lad and was soon close enough to be aware of the lingering smell of tobacco in the air.

Robert opened his mouth to call out when abruptly he felt that he was being watched.

103

It was the same sensation he had experienced at Sean Moidart's lecture the previous evening.

Pulling out his handkerchief he stopped and blew his nose. As he did so he glanced around him. There were several people strolling about the North Inch including a number of lads kicking a football, but all seemed intent on their own business.

It was really rather a peaceful scene with the mid-morning sun in a cloudless sky, and the River Tay flowing placidly by and gulls describing leisurely circles above the trees. Even the sound of traffic was only a distant hum. It was such an innocent picture that he almost failed to notice how the old man turned his back sharply on him and appeared to be studying the riverbank. Robert had just caught the movement out of the corner of his eye. Was there something vaguely familiar about the figure, something that made him feel uneasy?

Abruptly he turned and began to retrace his steps along the path. Back at the end of the road he saw the pavements were empty. Further along, on the opposite side, an open sportscar was reversing into a drive, while in the distance he could see the small van waiting to go out onto the main road. Nothing sinister in any of that, he thought. As for Benjamin, he should be able to look after himself. All the same he decided to retrace his steps and nip up the narrow path behind the house. Just in case . . .

But he needn't have bothered. The path was empty. Not a sign to be seen of either the Weasel or Benjamin. Oh well, he might as well return via the back garden. Seconds later he was pushing open the garden gate.

His eyes quickly took in the colourful herbaceous border and the trees on the right. Then he spotted the small figure in the deep shadow of the back of the house. He was trying to get in the back door which obviously Fiona had locked as instructed.

'Hey what's the problem?' he called out.

Benjamin turned towards him. 'I've been knocking and knocking b-but there's n-no reply.'

Robert shrugged casually. 'Perhaps she's in the loo or in the living-room. You know it's sometimes difficult to hear anything from the back of the house.'

Benjamin looked unconvinced. 'I h-hope she's all right.'

'Of course she is. Now don't worry.' And running up to the door Robert banged loudly on it.

'Hurry up, Sis,' he called out.

But the knocking echoed emptily through the old house.

And there was no sound of footsteps.

'Heck, this is ridiculous,' he grumbled. 'We'll just have to go round the side of the house and ring the bell.'

The bell rang loud and clear and then its sound became muffled in the recesses of Arisaig. Robert and Benjamin looked at each other in growing alarm.

'I just don't get it,' Robert said, trying the door handle. 'It's still locked so where's she got to in a few minutes.'

Benjamin's expression was lugubrious. 'As soon as the W-Weasel saw me he turned and s-seemed to be speaking into that stereo of his. And honest, Robert, it just looked as if he was giving instructions to someone. He p-pretended not to hear me calling to him and just walked away.'

Robert rubbed his chin, then as a breeze flickered through the garden and pulled at the living-room curtains, he noticed for the first time that the window was still wide open. He let out a strangled gasp.

'We never closed the window.'

In a second he had a leg over the sill and had dropped onto the carpet. Another second and he was heaving Benjamin after him.

'Quick – you search upstairs,' he commanded.

The search was fast yet thorough: it yielded not a clue as to what had occurred in their brief absence. Robert felt sick in the pit of his stomach. If anything happened to Fiona . . .

Benjamin's eyes were suddenly large and round like damp pebbles behind the thick lenses.

'W-What are we going to do?' he cried.

Robert ground his feet into the carpet with frustration. 'Well, one thing's for sure: it will be no good going round to the McLarnty's. That's the last place they'll have taken her.'

He looked indecisively out of the window at the empty street, recalling the blue van crawling along the pavement. 'There's nothing for it but to phone the police,' he stated heavily.

Benjamin, relieved that Robert had decided on a course of action, nodded his head enthusiastically. 'Yes let's do that.'

But strangely enough when Robert picked up the phone the line went abruptly dead. He stared in disbelief at the receiver, banged it against the palm of his hand and listened again.

'That's odd,' he remarked. 'There seems to be a fault. Oh well, we'll just have to go round to the police station.'

'But first, Robert, we'll have to close the window.' And the young lad bounded off into the living-room.

A second later Robert heard him call out in alarm.

'Robert!'

He raced through the half-open door to find Benjamin, the curtains blowing round his head, leaning through the open window.

'He's there on the other side of the road.'

Robert was across the room in an instant and peering out of the window. It was the Weasel, half-crouching in the shadow of the opposite wall and there was no doubt about it: he was speaking as if to himself, the stereo headphones clamped firmly over his skeletal head.

Anger erupted in Robert's mind like a torrential wave. Cursing to himself, he jerked Benjamin back from the window and prepared to leap out into the garden.

It was then that the phone rang. Robert stopped, one foot on the windowsill, and turned towards Benjamin. 'Did you hear that?'

Benjamin nodded, his expression perplexed. 'But the phone, it's out of order.'

Robert glanced back out of the window and across the road.

But the Weasel was nowhere to be seen. Once again the road was empty and silent.

Behind them the phone continued to ring, the sound reverberating harshly throughout the house. Slowly he turned and walked across the living-room into the hall. For a moment he stood gazing at the phone, frightened to lift the receiver. Benjamin had joined him and his eyes too were fastened on the black instrument which looked strangely menacing.

Finally Robert stretched out his hand to the receiver. As he did so the ringing stopped and silence hung heavy in the hall. He lifted the receiver. The line was dead.

'Come on, Benjamin,' he called taking the spare front door key from the chest of drawers.

But they had not even reached the front door when the phone rang again. This time

Robert wheeled round, took four steps across the hall, grabbed the receiver and put it to his ear.

At first there was only silence, then a sighing like the sough of the wind on a winter's night. He realised with growing fear that it was someone breathing. The words, when they came, were spoken in a harsh whisper that sent a shiver down his spine.

'I wouldn't go to the police if I were you. It would be a grave mistake.'

Robert butted in angrily. 'Who are you?' he demanded, though he knew already that it had to be the Whisperer.

The laugh was a rasp across the eardrums. 'You will know soon enough. In the meantime I want to be sure you understand my instructions. No calling the police, Robert, or Fiona will regret it for the rest of her life.'

Anguished, Robert called out. 'No. You mustn't touch her.'

Another rasp of a laugh and now the whisper seemed to swell in volume so that it filled the hall and echoed eerily up the winding staircase.

'Don't ever again try to give me orders, Robert. Do you understand?'

Robert was badly shaken. Weakly he gasped 'yes' because there was nothing else he dared do at that moment.

There was silence at the other end of the line and Robert fiddled with the phone for something to do while he waited to hear what the Whisperer had to say next. He glanced down at Benjamin. The face was paler than he had ever seen it, the eyes wide with fear, and his hands constantly toyed with the yo-yo.

'Robert,' the whisper was so low that it caught him unawares. 'Now you're going to do exactly what I tell you.' The voice became more peremptory. 'You do understand, don't you?'

Again Robert could only manage a weak 'yes'.

'Excellent. You and Benjamin will stay on the premises all day. Neither of you will try and make any contact with the rest of the world. Is that clear?'

'Yes.'

'And if you have the slightest doubt in your mind about that let me warn you that you will be under constant observation throughout the day. Any breach of my instruction will lead to instant retribution. Not on you, Robert, but on your delightful sister.'

Robert's grip on the receiver tightened. But he said nothing.

'When I am satisfied that you have learned to obey my instructions I will contact you again.'

The last rasping syllable had barely faded into the ether when the phone went dead. Once more they were cut off from contact with anyone else.

Benjamin was screwing up his eyes in an effort to hold back threatening tears. He tried a lopsided sort of smile.

'So we are under s-siege.'

'I reckon so, Numbers.'

'What are we to do?'

Robert glared at the receiver with sudden distaste and slammed it down on its cradle. 'I'm damned if I know.' Then to try and reassure the younger lad he added, 'But I'll think of something.'

That was at 12.35 p.m. By 5.30 p.m. when they sat down to an early supper of cold salad he had still not thought of anything. Worry and waiting had made him increasingly irritable and as he hunched over a cup of tea poor Benjamin sat miserable and silent at the other end of the kitchen table. Every time he tried to suggest anything Robert snapped his head off.

106

Even so Benjamin insisted on asking. 'But wh-what about Aunt Isobel. Wouldn't she phone us?'

'If she could,' replied Robert sourly, 'but she'll probably just think the blasted line's out of order.'

'I s-suppose so.'

Robert saw the crumpled expression on the youngster's face and felt sorry for him. 'Sorry, Benjamin. I've been rotten to you. But I'm really worried about Fiona.'

Benjamin's expression brightened slightly. 'That's all right Robert. I understand.'

Robert smiled back at him, suddenly glad to have his companionship: all day Arisaig had seemed empty and silent but that silence was broken less than five minutes later by the phone ringing. Robert was out of his chair in a flash and, running into the hall, grabbed the receiver.

'Hello, yes,' he called.

Tantalising silence greeted him.

'Hello, is there anyone there?'

The answering whisper set his nerves on edge. 'There's always someone there,' replied the voice.

Then there was a click and once more the phone went dead. Robert let the receiver fall back onto the cradle and stared with unseeing eyes towards the front door. He must have stood there for fully a minute. Gradually his eyes focussed as grimly he forced his anxieties into the back of his mind.

Joining him, Benjamin looked with horrified fascination in the direction of the door. He pointed a shaking hand towards it.

'L-Look,' he said in a half-whisper. 'The handle . . .'

Robert looked. The handle was turning slowly up and down as though someone wanted to enter the house. Benjamin backed away. Robert stood his ground and waited. The silence was almost unbearable but neither spoke.

A long thin manilla envelope slid through the letter box and fell to the ground.

Still neither of them moved nor spoke. Then, crossing the hall Robert bent down and cautiously picked it up. The writing, sharp and spikey, was in black ink. Ripping it open he scanned the contents.

The single sheet of paper, folded once, bore no address. The wording was as follows:

You have knowledge which you must share with me. If you are greedy and attempt to keep it to yourself your sister will suffer. But co-operate and she will be released unhurt.

Ignore this warning at your peril.

To prove that she is in good health I enclose a message from her.

I will issue my instructions to you in precisely six hours.

Remember my voice is only a whisper but it carried power throughout the land. Run as swiftly as you may, you will never escape me.

Do not try.

Instinctively Robert looked at his watch. It was exactly six o'clock. So the message would come at midnight. A creep of fear slithered down his spine but the best way to combat fear was action. He leaped forward, tore open the door and rushed out onto the path.

The front gate was still swinging on its hinges. Otherwise there was no indication that anyone had come to the door . . .

Chapter 21
THE FINAL CLUE

*Robert's enemy, the Whisperer, with a voice
like dead leaves scratching across gravel*

R obert felt sick with worry. Fiona was in grave danger and there seemed to be
nothing he could do about it. It was obvious too that Arisaig was under constant
observation.

Turning, he dragged his feet into the house and locked the door behind him. He
handed the waiting Benjamin the note and then looked inside the manilla envelope. A
small piece of paper was folded inside. Carefully he withdrew it, realising that it must
be the note from Fiona.

> Hey Rob, you know me well – I guess I still need educating because I'm
> in trouble with the Black Bishops for the sixth time. Still it's nice to be able
> to play chess if nothing else.
> I'm alive and well and hoping they let me free. But that depends on you
> Rob. Please do what they say or they won't let me home.
> Lots of love
> Fiona.
> PS I'm sorry I was so silly stupid and forgot to close the window and
> caused you all this bother.

Robert silently handed Fiona's note to Benjamin and, knuckling his eyes, slouched
miserably into the kitchen where he sat at the table, head in hands.

He felt Benjamin's hand on his arm. He shrugged it off.

'Leave me alone,' he muttered.

'But Robert,' protested Benjamin, 'there's a c-clue here.'

Robert, not in the mood for playing amateur detectives, squeezed his eyes shut, while
his hands clenched and unclenched spasmodically.

'Listen, why should she write all this about chess?'

He looked up at the younger lad. 'Oh you know Fiona, trying to cheer herself and us
up.'

Benjamin was doubtful. 'The end doesn't sound like that. And she's called you Rob.'

108

'That's just to warn me – Beware of Rat.'

'Is she often in trouble with the black bishops?'

'Not that I can remember.'

'And what about this needing educating?' Benjamin's eyes were serious behind his glasses and for a moment he looked much older than his years.

'I still think she's trying to tell us something.'

'All right, bright spark, tell me what it is.'

Benjamin's face puckered then his brow furrowed in concentration.

'What's a bishop and why has it got a capital letter?'

Robert felt too wretched to respond with any enthusiasm.

'A bishop's a dignitary in the Church of England.'

Benjamin shook his head. 'No another word, Robert.'

'A minister, a priest,' suggested Robert.

'Black minister, black priest.' Benjamin wandered absentmindedly across to the bowl of apples in the corner and polishing one on the seat of his trousers returned to the table.

'Got it,' he exclaimed. 'A black friar.'

Robert squirmed impatiently in his seat. 'Look Numbers, let's just leave it. Please.'

But now Benjamin's voice was eager, all trace of a stutter gone.

'Listen, she said black bishops. Now say black friars as one word.'

Understanding began to dawn in Robert's mind. 'Not, not Blackfriars.'

'Of course. It's only down the road. The whole of that area was known as Blackfriars in the old days because of the monastery. There was a piece in the *Perthshire Advertiser* when the Hydro Board were extending their offices and excavations revealed remains from the past.'

'So she's telling us she's somewhere in Blackfriars,' exclaimed Robert excitedly. 'But whereabouts?'

Benjamin was all eager enthusiasm. 'Here's the clue, Robert – educating.'

Robert puzzled his brains. 'I give up,' he said at last.

'The old Academy building in Rose Terrace.'

Robert was impressed. 'You are quick on the uptake, Numbers.'

The young lad flushed with pleasure and scrunched into his apple till his cheeks bulged.

'And you see they are converting the old school – I think it was used as Government offices or something for years – into l-luxury f-flats.'

'Converting you say,' Robert pounced on the word.

'Yes, they've only just begun so part of the building is unoccupied. I've been and had a look for myself.'

'Numbers, you're marvellous,' he exclaimed and pushing back the chair began to walk to and fro across the kitchen floor.

'Now what do we do?'

Benjamin smiled to himself. 'You'll think of something, Big White Chief.'

Once again that day Benjamin's faith in him touched Robert. He glanced at his watch. 'Five and a half hours to midnight when they are next going to contact us.' He looked out of the kitchen window. 'It's pretty dull out there. In fact we might even have a repeat of last night's fog if we're lucky.'

'So as soon as it's dark we creep out and nip along to Rose Terrace.'

Easier said than done,' replied Robert thoughtfully. 'But we'll manage somehow.'

'So wh-what do we do now?'

'Look at Fiona's note again for more clues.'

Benjamin pushed his glasses further up his nose and sitting down at the table studied

Fiona's artistic, though uneven writing. 'What do you make of this bit "in trouble with the Black Bishops for the sixth time?"'

Fiercely Robert massaged his chin. 'It's got to be something to do with the number. My guess is we'll find out later.'

Benjamin looked more owlish than ever. 'Yes I think so too.'

Robert studied the dirty dishes in the sink. 'Reckon we'd better clear up first.' If something happened to them he did not want Aunt Isobel returning to dirty dishes. That would be a pretty rotten epitaph, he thought to himself.

Eight o'clock and the phone rang. They had both been trying to concentrate on a game of draughts in the living-room and the harsh sound came as such a shock that as Benjamin leaped to his feet his hand caught the board and scattered the pieces all over the floor.

Glancing at his watch Robert thought it was odd that the Whisperer should ring early. It could mean disaster for their plan to try and rescue Fiona as soon as the mist thickened and darkness began to fall.

When he heard the voice at the other end of the line he could hardly believe it. 'Aunt Isobel,' he shouted. 'It's great to hear you.'

'Don't overdo it, Robert,' she remarked in some surprise. 'You knew I would phone sometime. In fact I tried earlier but the phone seemed to be engaged all the time. I couldn't think who you were talking to.'

For an instant Robert could not think what to say. 'It must have been a fault,' he began, desperately trying to think how he could warn Aunt Isobel of what had happened.

'Are you all right?' And without waiting for a reply she went on. 'I hope you've been feeding yourselves properly.'

'Oh yes. But Aunt Isobel,' he started.

However, he got no further because at that precise moment there was a strange whispering sound on the line. He could not make out the words but he knew with a feeling of dread that it was the Whisperer himself listening in.

'Yes dear. There's nothing wrong is there?'

The whispering grew louder, more insistent, more frightening.

'We seem to have a crossed line.' Her voice sounded fainter. His only link with the outside world was fading.

'Aunt Isobel,' he cried out. 'We're fine.'

The whispering became the faintest rustle of a breeze. Aunt Isobel's voice was loud and clear. 'Good. Well, Rosemary is making a remarkable recovery I am glad to say. So I should hope to be back with you all tomorrow afternoon.'

Robert just prayed that they would all be there. Benjamin, who had been standing just behind him, grabbed the phone. 'A thousand yippees,' he shouted.

She laughed. 'Now young man, no staying up late because I'm away.'

'No, Aunt Isobel,' he replied in a subdued voice.

'Well, love to you all. And tell Fiona that Oban would be marvellous for painting. There's a beautiful sunset tonight. See you tomorrow.'

They walked back into the living-room together, discussing the phone call.

'My guess is that the Whisperer knew she would ring and thought she might be worried if she could not get through to us.'

Benjamin nodded wisely.

*****

Robert had never thought he would pray for fog but he did that fateful evening. The first tendrils drifted in as ten o'clock struck and soon were thickening. The two of them had closed the thin curtains, put on table lamps and were about to switch on the TV when they heard a rustling sound outside the window.

Faintly silhouetted against the street light was the shadowy outline of a figure. It raised a hand and deliberately scratched a fingernail across the glass.

The two of them froze, their eyes drawn hypnotically to the curtained window. The screech of the fingernail had their nerves in tatters within seconds. Benjamin put a hand to his mouth. Robert gritted his teeth and waited to see what would happen next.

Then the hand waved a hideous sort of farewell and the figure merged back into the fog.

The warning had been given.

The next half an hour dragged by as they finalised their plans. Robert was to escape via the back door and then climb over the wall into the next garden. Benjamin in the meantime would remain at home in case the phone rang again.

They both crept into the kitchen and with the light out Robert silently pushed open the door and peered down the garden. The apple trees stood out in the grey light but the gate at the bottom of the garden was only a blur. He knew he would be in deep shadow so unless someone was watching closely he should be able to escape without being spotted.

Briefly he gripped Benjamin's hand, hoping that he was not leaving the lad in any danger, and then he stealthily tiptoed towards the wall. Carefully he climbed onto the coal bin and swung himself over the wall into the next garden.

Behind him he heard the door close. At least Benjamin was obeying instructions.

But Benjamin was far from obeying instructions: as soon as he had closed the door he ran into the hall and, lifting the telephone receiver off the hook, deliberately placed it on the dresser. Then he went into the living-room, turned up the volume of the TV and, collecting all the cushions from the various chairs, placed them on one chair which he angled towards the TV. Satisfied that someone glancing through the thin curtains would see a vague shape in the chair and naturally assume it was either Robert or himself, he left the room.

★★★★★

Robert stood for a few seconds while he got his bearings, then he was off across the garden and over the second wall in an instant. Only another two gardens and he reckoned he would be at the end of the lane and comparatively safe to emerge.

It was only when he did so that he realised that the fog was miraculously beginning to clear. The stars were already beginning to come out. It was going to be a fine night after all and that could spell disaster for him. But there was no turning back now. He had to go on – and fast.

There were several people in Rose Terrace and that worried him even more. One could easily be a look-out. He sought to reassure himself by thinking that they would hardly be expecting anyone and so would probably have taken no special precautions. Certainly not at this early hour.

Only at midnight would they become suspicious and by then he hoped to have spirited Fiona away.

Two cars drove slowly by. To his left a double-decker bus passed along Athol Street. Nothing could have seemed more normal. Yet somewhere in that cold grey building with the clock permanently stopped at seven minutes to two, Fiona was being held hostage. Now he took time to study her prison, the former Perth Academy.

While he did so a figure hid behind a nearby tree on the North Inch and kept him under surveillance.

111

The first thing that Robert noticed was that all the windows were blocked in with wood – the tall first-storey ones with dark wood, those on the ground floor with plywood bleached by the sun. There were two doors, green paint peeling off them, the lower half badly scuffed, with heavy black handles.

Quickly he looked up and down the street – still no one obviously suspicious in sight. He crossed the road and surreptitiously examined the first door. A brass padlock kept the bar across it firmly in place. He paced the length of the building to the next door: exactly thirty-six paces. Once a notice had been pinned up on the door, for there were still four drawing-pins stuck firmly in.

A figure detached itself from the tree and approached the building till it was directly opposite Robert.

But Robert's attention was on the number 6 at the top of the door. This must be what Fiona had been referring to. He glanced along the pavement and an instant later was pushing the door open.

★★★★★

Inside it was dark with a dank, musty smell in the air. He switched on his small pocket torch. There was a corridor ahead with a wide door at the end. Taking a deep breath, he plunged ahead till he reached the door. The handle turned easily and the door opened into a large hall. He extinguished the torch and stood and listened.

As he did so he began to realise how cold and bleak it was. The silence had a depth and texture that threatened to smother him. He felt he wanted to push it physically aside.

Behind him there was faint click as if a door had closed. He tensed, flattened his back against the wall and waited. Not another sound. He would have to be careful he told himself or his imagination would run away with him.

He went back into the corridor, flicking his torch beam along the floor and up a broad staircase covered in thick dust. His thoughts were grim. Dust-covered staircases were a dead giveaway: several sets of footsteps marched up the staircase. Bending down he decided that one set of prints was much smaller than the others.

Instinctively he looked upward but no one lurked there waiting for him. Obviously they felt secure. So they had not suspected Fiona's message conveyed any secret warning. At least then he would have the advantage of surprise.

Robert went up the stairs as quickly as he dared. Below a pair of watchful eyes watched every step he took.

Once on the landing he was confronted by a series of doors leading off a long corridor which itself divided into two halfway along. Obviously in the past these had led into classrooms. For a moment his mind went back to his schooldays in Jasper – bright modern classrooms and the open countryside only a cricket ball's throw away. He thought of his friends and wondered how Joe would have reacted had he seen him now. It seemed light years away and yet only weeks had passed since he had arrived in Scotland and left that life behind him for ever.

Everything had been different: even his name. Now he was a Kinlochy determined to discover his true identity and discover too his relationship with the Whisperer who was surely some phantom from his own past. It was an eerie, puzzling thought but he had to face it that perhaps a century earlier he might have been in this very building himself. If so he must certainly have fought against the Whisperer . . . but surely all that was imaginative nonsense?

He groaned inwardly as he started trying the doors one by one. He still had no proof that anyone by the name of Kinlochy had ever even existed. On their own, the napkin rings were insufficient proof.

112

He simply had to find some other evidence to show that it was worth continuing his search.

Behind him a lone figure crept warily up the stairs . . .

Masters' studies, classrooms redolent with the atmosphere of past generations of school children, all were there as he opened door after door. It was like stepping into the past but without the benefit of a guide.

In the classrooms the woodwork, inkstained and discoloured, was covered in carved initials. Crudely drawn hearts with arrows through them and names like Bill and Susie, Jean and Peter, bore evidence of long forgotten romances.

But nowhere was there any sign of Fiona or her captors. Anxiety began to build up in Robert till he found himself sweating. He had to find her, if it was the last thing he did. Spurred on by the need to rescue his sister he grew impatient, let his torch stray further ahead of him than was prudent, scuffed his feet against loose boards . . .

And all the time only a few feet behind him followed the unseen figure, crouching low so that if Robert turned abruptly he would not at once be noticed.

Robert began to realise that the building was bigger than the thirty-six paces had indicated: the estimate had given him no indication of how far it stretched back from Rose Street. He stopped and, shielding his torch beam, looked at his watch. Already nearly 11.30 p.m. It was taking him longer than he had imagined. Time was running short.

He plunged quickly on, heedless of any noise he might make.

The bright swiftly-moving pool of light from a large torch suddenly appeared as if from nowhere directly ahead of him. It grew round, elongated, pencil-thin and then round again as it sprayed its light across floor and walls.

Robert froze. He had turned off his own torch instantly and was in total darkness. His own breathing and the banging of his heart were so loud that he did not hear the involuntary gasp behind him.

The voice came from within the recesses of a huge upstairs classroom. It was only a whisper, no more, but it echoed with eerie intensity throughout the room and the corridor in which Robert stood.

The shock was almost too much to bear. He leaned against the wall and closed his eyes as he had done as a child when he had hoped to hide himself. Perhaps too he subconsciously wanted to shut out the image of the alien torch beam and of that awful whisper.

He succeeded with the torch beam but the echo of the whisper seemed to gather in volume, thrown back from wall to wall, till like a huge ball of sound, it moved inexorably down the corridor towards him.

'What is happening out there, Bill? Who is it?' A sinister note entered the Whisperer's voice. 'Remember no evidence must be left. Not a single scrap.'

Footsteps ahead. But Robert was too scared to open his eyes. Briefly he saw against his eyelids a brilliant flash of light. He cringed further back, making his outline as small as possible.

'We cannot be too careful tonight.' A moment's silence. 'I shall be making the phone-call shortly.'

Involuntarily Robert shivered. He opened his eyes and saw a huge shadow looming ahead of him. It turned and disappeared through the door. Robert began to breathe more easily. He tiptoed forward, his torchlight shaded so that he could only see a foot ahead at a time. Progress was slow but eventually he reached the door.

Behind him a silent figure reached into its pocket and pulled out something which could have been a weapon. Then it closed up on Robert with every appearance of being ready to strike.

Robert's foot struck something on the floor and momentarily he stumbled and nearly lost his balance. At the other side of the doorway less than a yard away someone let out an oath and the searching torch beam carved through the darkness.

Robert dropped to his knees and remained motionless. A second later the torch beam was switched off and he was back in the anonymous darkness again. He ran his free hand along the floor till it came in contact with a loose half brick.

Carefully he hefted it in his hand, getting used to the weight and feel of it. Here was a weapon with deadly potential. He could not afford to be squeamish in how he used it . . .

Robert, alert to the slightest warning sound of danger, crept forward.

When he reached the doorway he halted in surprise. In front of him was a vast room with a narrow winding staircase leading up to the bell tower. In the far left corner, next to a heavy duty portable lamp and a single battered school desk, sat a vaguely recognisable figure smoking a cigar. Black hair sleeked back, dark moustache, high cheekbones, eyes black as the entrance to hell.

This surely must be the Whisperer himself, the Phantom from the Past. Only later was Robert to learn that he was a master of disguises for all his saturnine features. In minutes, rubber pouches in his cheeks would change the whole contour of his face . . . a curly auburn wig and he was a transformed person.

But at this moment, hidden from the prying eyes of the rest of the world, he was himself, totally in command of the situation – or so he thought, decided Robert grimly. He stood just back from the doorway in deep shadow and studied his arch enemy. So intent was he on doing so that he had forgotten all about the presence of the other man, Bill.

Robert, brick still in hand, took two steps forward into the former classroom.

From high above, perched in the lonely bell tower, there came a shriek of warning. 'Watch your right, Rob!'

Verbal messages to the brain take a millisecond to register. Action takes a fraction longer. In this case the delay was greater because his mind was registering that it was Fiona who had called to him telling him that she was alive and up in the bell tower.

In that instant a brawny figure launched himself at him, hands outstretched to grab him by the throat.

But Robert's reflexes were fast. He whirled round smashing the brick up and across against his antagonist's right shoulder. There was a sickening thud and, writhing in agony, the man crashed to the floor.

Now Robert's only thought was to reach Fiona. Torch held high in his left hand he sprinted across the room heedless of the Whisperer uncoiling like a snake from his wooden chair. Too late he turned to face his new foe.

A clenched fist caught his armpit and pain shot through his body. He reeled back and the Whisperer was onto him. But somehow he mustered sufficient strength to strike out. He hit his assailant on the chest, winding him.

Unknown to Robert the Whisperer's strength lay not in his body but in the subtlety and evil nature of his mind. His was a mental power infinitely more dangerous than mere physical strength.

Now his reaction was to reach his captive in the bell tower and with her held physical hostage he knew Robert would capitulate and promise anything for her freedom.

Calculating in this way he spun round and leapt for the staircase. High up above him Fiona, now bound hand and foot, cringed back in terror.

Robert tripped and crashed to the ground, the pain from the Whisperer's blow now so intense that he could not move.

114

It was as if he had been paralysed. Groaning, he tried to struggle to a sitting position but failed.

Now the Whisperer had glanced behind him and, seeing that Robert was immobilised, sneered.

'Such puny strength. You should know that I can only be defeated by intellectual power and cunning.'

The whispering voice echoed from wall to wall, floor to ceiling, strangely exaggerated by the design of the bell tower – a fact known to past generations of schoolchildren who had been educated in the old Perth Academy.

Summoning every ounce of his strength Robert gradually began to force himself to his feet.

Hastily the Whisperer turned and began to climb up towards Fiona.

It was then that it all happened and with such speed that Robert could not credit his senses.

In one moment the old classroom with its host of carved initials, the lone desk, ink-stained and battered, near where the Whisperer had been sitting, the lamp illuminating one corner, Fiona's pale frightened face peering down at him, were all engraved like a painting on his mind.

The next moment a small, stocky whirlwind figure was bounding up from behind him. In his hand was the yo-yo with which he had developed such an uncanny accuracy.

Benjamin may have had a speech impediment and thick lensed glasses which made him the butt of schoolfellows but they did not affect that skill with the yo-yo.

He reached the bottom of the staircase, arched his body well to the left and then up zipped the yo-yo. It travelled so fast that Robert could not follow it. One moment it was in Benjamin's hand. The next it had spun round the Whisperer's ankles.

Benjamin stood back, jerked on the high-strength nylon cord and, with a scream of rage, the Whisperer came cartwheeling through the air. His head smashed to the floor where he lay senseless.

Back beside the door Bill was also motionless, having fainted from the sheer pain of the blow from the brick.

Robert felt like crying aloud with joy.

'Good old Numbers,' he shouted hoarsely as he staggered forward.

Benjamin, turning, flashed him a cheeky grin, and then was climbing the stairs.

The worst of the pain began to ease away and by the time Benjamin had reached Fiona and untied the cord binding her, he was able to walk to the foot of the stairs.

'Mac,' the relief in that one word was enormous. 'Oh it's wonderful to see you.' Then she added quickly. 'And Benjamin our hero.'

Up in the confined space of the bell tower Benjamin still managed a little war dance, bowing and shaking hands with himself, so that Fiona and Robert cried with laughter.

'Come on down, Sis, and let's get moving out of here.'

'No – not yet.'

Robert looked up at the peaked, pale face in surprise. 'Why on earth not?'

'Because I have found something you simply must see.'

Robert's hand was on the narrow balustrade. Exhausted he leaned his head against his arm.

'I can't,' he muttered.

'You must or you are no Kinlochy,' she called back.

Hearing the name, he straightened up. 'What do you mean?' he cried.

'Come and see for yourself.'

Each step took every ounce of courage he had left. But finally he reached Fiona and

Benjamin. The light from the heavy-duty lamp below filtered dimly up into the narrow bell tower. Below and around them everything was shifting shadows.

Even now the menace of the Whisperer stretched its tentacles out towards them. Robert realised that they must escape quickly and yet here he was deliberately going further into the trap.

He shone the now faint beam from his torch around the bell tower thinking – or was it remembering – the shattering, mindnumbing sound of the bell in the old days as the clock struck the hour.

Then he saw that Fiona was pointing a slender hand, usually white and manicured, now grimy with dust, nails broken as she had tried to free herself from the binding ropes.

'Read that, Mac, and never again doubt or forget who you are.'

With a strange sense of having experienced all this long, long ago, he leaned forward. The writing on the single pine-wood post was vaguely familiar. Later Fiona was to point out that it bore an uncanny resemblance to his own.

But at that moment his whole attention was concentrated on the words – KINLOCHY WAS HERE.

Slowly Robert straightened his shoulders and a smile crossed his face. So there had been a Kinlochy and right here where he stood.

He felt he had discovered the first part of his destiny.

Now the Quest was on in earnest. It might take months, years, but he would persevere however the Whisperer might conspire to thwart his efforts.

'Kinlochy!' He roared out the name in the dark, shadow-strewn bell tower and it echoed up and down and round the classroom, growing ever louder.

Even when that cry was but a memory, its force still seemed to echo on, gathering strength and momentum to propel Robert forward.

Benjamin whipped out his yo-yo and sent it
arching up towards the Whisperer's legs

116

THE PHANTOM CLAYMORE

Now watch out for the exciting sequel, *The Phantom Claymore*.

Peering into the gathering night Robert's eyes play tricks on him. Trees, bushes take on lurking shapes of human figures. At other times he thinks he can hear someone. Footsteps and breathing ahead and behind him . . .

Then over to his left something moving – travelling parallel to himself. He halts and the figure halts too. He begins to climb and the other figure is a mirror image.

Mist, growing darkness, deepening fear, all contribute to distorting sound and vision. What if the *searchers* catch him? That would be the end of the Quest, possibly the end of the Kinlochys . . .

DON'T MISS HOW ROBERT CONTINUES HIS BATTLE WITH THE EVIL MENACE OF THE WHISPERER. IT'S ALL IN *THE PHANTOM CLAYMORE*!